Cougars
And
Cradle
Robbers

Cougars And Cradle Robbers

From the Editors
Of *True Story* And
True Confessions

Published by True Renditions, LLC

True Renditions, LLC
105 E. 34th Street, Suite 141
New York, NY 10016

ISBN: 978-1-938877-80-3

Visit us on the web at www.truerenditionsllc.com.

Contents

CRADLE ROBBER
Seduced By My Daughter's Man!

My daughter, Reagan and I, are only fifteen years apart, so some people mistake us for sisters when we go out shopping. I admit it pleases me whenever someone thinks we're the same age, but I'm not always sure Reagan appreciates the comments.

I had Reagan when I was just a sophomore in high school. Reagan's daddy was a friend of my older brother—a guy who had been around our home ever since I could remember. I always liked Maxwell.

Maxwell and my brother, Frank, were six years older than me, but Maxwell always called me gorgeous, and he always paid special attention to me. When I became a teenager, Maxwell spent lots of time with me while waiting for my brother to get ready. Frank was always late—for everything.

Maxwell started to come over just to see me—long after Frank had left for the service. We would sit out on the porch on summer nights and tell each other all our hopes and dreams. Maxwell was very gentle, not like the boys at school, who were always cracking dirty jokes and treated me with disrespect. Maxwell was different; he was a real gentleman.

We started to take rides in Maxwell's car, and my parents didn't seem to mind. They considered Maxwell as one in the family. Eventually, we started to park and make out, but Maxwell was never in a hurry like the other guys I'd dated. He had a slow hand. He took his time, driving me crazy with his deep kisses and soft caresses. It wasn't long before I fell in love with him.

Eventually, our kisses and hugs turned into more serious business, and one night after swimming in the lake, we climbed into the back seat of Maxwell's roomy car, and I found myself nude for the first time in front of a man. Maxwell told me how beautiful I was, and before I knew it, he was inside of me. Oh, it hurt at first, but by the second time, I was crying out for more!

"Hey, baby, you've got to kill that noise or someone will hear us!" Maxwell warned.

I couldn't help it, I was absolutely crazy about Maxwell and I was just overwhelmed by having his naked body on top of mine. I waited for Maxwell to call after that night, but he didn't. I was confused, and after about a week, I called his house and his mother told me he had left for the army, and he wouldn't be home for a long time.

I cried myself to sleep for many nights after that, but those nights were nothing compared to the unhappiness I experienced when I learned I was pregnant. I didn't even realize it until I was about four months along. I was such a stupid kid. My periods had often been irregular, and somehow, I didn't think you could get pregnant just after one night of sex. I guess I thought it took more times or something, because I didn't worry for a while, until my pants started getting tight and I started getting terrible morning sickness. I couldn't figure out what kind of flu went away every afternoon and came back every morning.

My mother figured it out after having two pregnancies of her own. She was the one who made me face the possibility.

"Bibi, honey, I'm not going to mince words. I'm going to tell you up front. All that throwing up in the morning that I hear you doing, even if you try to keep it secret, is worrying me. And I see your waist isn't slim and trim like it used to be. I 'm afraid we're going to have to take a trip to the doctor and see what's going on," she said."

"Oh, Mama, nothing's wrong with me," I whined, trying to throw her off course. "I just got the flu. I'll be okay."

But Mama insisted. The doctor called us both in his office, and he informed us that I was pregnant. I was more humiliated than I had even been in my life. I refused to tell anyone who the father was, and finally, everyone stopped asking. Even if they suspected Maxwell, no one said anything.

I dropped out of school and took night classes until Reagan was born. I took a course that trained me to be a legal secretary, and I was able to support the two of us in our own apartment. Mama babysat Reagan, and that enabled me to save a little money.

Reagan was an easy baby, and one of the prettiest babies I'd ever seen. Her daddy never did come by our house, again, and he wouldn't have been able to recognize Reagan as his own because she looked exactly like me.

I used to fantasize that Maxwell would be back to marry me, but I heard from my brother that he married someone in the service and lived in Korea. His mother and father had moved, so he never came back to our town.

Reagan asked about her daddy when she started school, and I told her he had died before she was born. I found a nicely framed picture of a handsome young man at an antique store, and I told her that he was her father. She seemed to accept my story, and reluctantly, my family went along.

After Reagan was in junior high school, I got married to a rich, handsome man. I was sick and tired of struggling to make ends meet. I'd been through a lot, and I felt that I deserved the good life, and I'd move heaven and earth to have it. So Tariq and his megabucks seemed like the answer for Reagan and me.

Tariq was an entrepreneur of a boutique, and he always had a nice suit on and a wallet full of money. But he also had a gambling problem, but I didn't know about that when I married him. My mother suspected that something was wrong with Tariq, but I wouldn't listen.

We were married about a year, and at first everything was fine. Tariq wasn't too thrilled about Reagan, but he seemed to tolerate her. Reagan was afraid of him—especially when he was in a foul mood, and he'd start yelling. She'd never been around such an angry man. My father was a quiet, easy man, so she just couldn't understand Tariq's temper.

But Tariq was always in a foul mood after losing money playing spades or poker or betting the horses. Not only did he lose his money, but the savings I had struggled so long to accumulate, began to dwindle.

One night, Tariq hit me, and that was the end. I packed my bags and moved to my mother's house— even though we were still living in my apartment. Eventually, Tariq left town, and I moved back to my apartment. Tariq had managed to tear it up during one of his bad moods when he flew into a rage for some unknown reason. It took me nearly six months to get it back to normal.

After my awful experience with Tariq, I swore off men for a long time. Oh, I dated some, going out with guys my nosey friends arranged for me, but what I had gone through with Maxwell and Tariq closed my heart to men. I wanted a perfect man, and none of the guys I ran into, came anywhere near to fitting my standards for someone I wanted to spend the rest of my life with.

When Reagan entered high school, I was so scared that the same thing that happened to me would happen to her. No one could tell me that history wouldn't repeat itself. I couldn't help it, but I just had to protect her. I couldn't bear to go through it again with my child. It would be even more painful to see my darling daughter be used. I just couldn't let it happen.

Reagan was a very beautiful teenager, with a lean body, and beautiful light brown eyes. Her hair was soft and wavy, and she had a smile that would light up the room when she came in. She was an excellent student, did well in every subject, and she had a chance for a volleyball scholarship. My Reagan was a superstar; she was going places, and no testosterone-driven man was going to screw up things for her like they did for me!

Of course, young men flocked to our home like bees to honey, although some of them were easily half Reagan's height. It didn't seem to matter. Guys were really turned on by Reagan.

I kept Reagan busy with all sorts of activities and studying; and I forbade her to date at all until she was sixteen. She became very rebellious many times before her sixteenth birthday, accusing me of being the worst mother in the world who wanted to spoil her life. She just didn't seem to understand that my strict standards were going to save her life!

"Mama," she would say to me crying. "You are so unfair to me. I hate you."

After her sixteenth birthday, Reagan announced that she would be dating frequently, and there was nothing I could do about it. She was very headstrong—just like me. She was eager to have boyfriends after waiting so long. Some of her friends had dated for five years already! Two of them were also pregnant, I always added, hoping she'd face reality.

Reagan had good taste in boys—most of the time—not going out with the scrubs or chickenheads who always seemed to hang around. Reagan was in all of the college prep courses, so her friends were serious-minded kids with aspirations for making something out of their lives. I have to admit that I even liked a few of her young men, especially one named Jared, whose mother was a friend of mine.

"Reagan, why don't you invite Jared over for dinner some night soon?" I asked, hoping she'd take my suggestion.

I could see Reagan was pleased I wasn't fighting her about dating anymore. But she explained that nothing had really come of their romance.

"'Jared is just too much of a square, but I met a guy I really like named Vincent. Could I have him over?"

With reluctance, I agreed. I was sorry to see Jared disappear from the scene so soon. In my heart, I felt that she was making a big mistake and by the time she'd realized it, he'd be long gone into another girl's arms.

The minute I set eyes on Vincent when he walked into my house, I knew that he was trouble with a capital T!

Sexual energy filled the house as Vincent sauntered toward me, and I found myself responding to his extraordinary good looks. It had been such a long time since I'd been with a man, saving all my energy for my job and Reagan—not wanting to be hurt again. I was disgusted with myself to be attracted to Vincent's bare arms, revealing bulging muscles, and his tight leather pants clinging to his rock hard thigh muscles.

However, when Vincent let out a wolf whistle and spoke to me, my instant attraction turned to irritation.

"Hey, Mama, you are fine! I can see why Reagan is so good-looking."

I could see immediately that this young man was a disaster waiting to happen. He was a typical smooth operator type, like many of the men in my life I had been attracted to. He was a guy who'd always mean heartbreak, and sometimes, even catastrophe. Vincent represented everything I had worried about all these years for Reagan, my beautiful daughter with a wonderful future in front of her. If only I could protect her from the Vincents of the world . . .

It was so painful to watch the same pattern happening over and over again to young girls I had known, and of course in my own experience as well. It was hard to understand why so many wonderful, bright girls found themselves attracted to such creatures. I had to admit that Vincent was physically attractive, and I'm sure Reagan responded to his looks as well. Maybe it also was the desire to reform, or to see what exactly was so sweet about forbidden fruit. When would she ever learn?

I could barely be civil to Vincent, although Reagan was completely unaware of how I was feeling. I could see in her eyes that she had fallen for Vincent, and I couldn't stand to watch.

I asked a few questions at dinner to try to appear civil.

"Vincent, what do you do?"

"I work at a gas station, Mrs. Newell, or can I call you by your first name?" he answered flippantly.

"Do you plan to work at a gas station your whole life?" I asked, ignoring his arrogance and ignorance.

I noticed Reagan glaring at me, probably thinking that I should like the creep calling me by my first name.

"Well, I don't know. I just take one day at a time and see what happens. Who knows, we could all be killed tomorrow!"

The ultimate cop-out, I thought. This young man was only living for now. He will make Reagan a terrible husband and a dreadful father for her children. How can I make her see that?

After Vincent went home, Reagan burst into my room, and yelled at me full throttle.

"Mother, you were so mean to Vincent. He didn't do anything to deserve your rudeness! I really feel sorry for him! He really has no family, and he really wanted you to like him. You apologize to him when he comes over again!"

"Reagan, Vincent is the kind of guy who can ruin your life. Take it from me . . . I know. I've been around guys like him. He's not the kind of guy that girls as special as you should be around!"

"Why, does he remind you of my daddy?" She snapped. "Did my daddy hurt you like you think Vincent and every other guy in the world is going to hurt me? When are you ever going to let me live my own life?"

I couldn't believe how cruel Reagan was being. I could see that she was already hooked on Vincent, and I had to do something

5

immediately to stop it. Fighting it head on was just not going to work with someone as strong-willed as Reagan. I had to think of a plan to save my little girl from making the biggest mistake of her life.

I decided not to fight Vincent openly, but to just wait until I could figure out a plan to get rid of him.

"Mother, I appreciate your apologizing to Vincent. He feels a lot better, now. You'll see; he is really a great guy!"

Great guy . . . sure! Vincent was as sleazy and lowdown as my ex-husband, Tariq.

Reagan saw him with rose-colored glasses, but I saw him clearly. When I came home after a hard day's work and find Vincent with his feet up on our coffee table, my blood boiled.

"Hi, Bibi, what's up in the working world?" he asked.

I was always tempted to reply with some sarcastic remark like, "You wouldn't know, would you?" especially in light of the fact Vincent had lost his job at the gas station. Reagan made excuses for him and tried to convince me that his boss was unfair. I was willing to bet anything that Vincent was simply too trifling to work!

Guys like Vincent always had trouble with people in authority. They always blamed everyone else for their failures. Someone was always out to get them. Vincent talked about everyone hassling him . . . teachers making him quit school . . . Vincent was never responsible for his misfortune.

What in the world did Reagan see in him? I wondered, but knowing how real life worked, she'd probably gotten a taste of decent loving and had lost her mind. My baby was probably "whupped!"

I had to admit, the sight of Vincent, at times, not only annoyed me, but sometimes, I felt turned on—much to my dismay. Vincent was always dressed so fly, even though he didn't seem to have a job or any family. I suspected that he was probably dealing drugs on top of all of his other terrible traits.

I kept my suspicions secret, and I continued to be civil to Vincent, hurrying out of the room as fast as my feet would take me so I'd avoid the confusing emotions I always felt when I saw Vincent. I was getting more worried as I saw Reagan falling head over heels for him. I had to come up with a plan—fast!

Reagan didn't know it, but she'd given me an idea several days later when she came home all upset over her best friend, Gerri's, terrible problem.

"You won't believe what happened to Gerri! She found her boyfriend in bed with another girl. She and Ted had planned to be married! I'm so mad at Ted. That's one thing I would never put up with in a guy . . . infidelity! If I ever found out Vincent was unfaithful to me, or even came on to another girl, that'd be the end!"

Never say never, darling daughter, I thought. Instinctively, I knew that Vincent had a roving eye. He was always coming on to me, probably knowing full well I found him attractive. Some men just knew those things. Reagan never seemed to notice, but I sure did. What if I encourage him to come back? Will Reagan notice his behavior then?

The next night when Vincent came over, I was waiting in the living room for him. When Reagan went to her room to get something, I sat down next to Vincent, pretending to take a real interest in him.

"Well, Vincent, how is life treating you these days?" I asked him in a very friendly tone of voice.

"Oh, all right. I looked for a job, but I think my old boss put the word not to hire me. I seem to get by in spite of everything, though."

"Yeah, you always seem to be so well-dressed. It's nice to have a handsome guy like you around the house."

I could see that Vincent was getting a bit confused by my attention. He shifted nervously and squirmed in his seat.

"I really don't understand why you don't have more boyfriends around, Bibi. You're a beautiful older honeydip . . . you should have guys falling all over you," Vincent said, uneasily.

"Oh, I guess I'm pretty picky about my men. I like them young and lean—like you."

With that comment, Vincent's eyes began to light up. I could see that he was finally convinced that I was serious, and I saw suspicion disappear from his face. Opportunity dawned on him.

Just then, Reagan came back into the room with a huge smile on her face and news about a hip-hop concert she had just seen in the paper. I got up and left, saying goodnight particularly nicely to Vincent. I knew I had begun the ball rolling. Now, I just had to figure out how to trap Vincent and take my scheme to the next level so Reagan would see what an unfaithful dog he really was.

The next day at work, I found the way. There was a small tape recorder in my desk drawer. I could hide it under the couch one night when I was talking to Vincent. I could send Reagan out on an errand and have Vincent to myself. Then, I could really prove to Reagan that Vincent had a roving eye. I knew it was risky, but so was the possibility of Reagan getting pregnant by that horrible young man.

A few nights later, I knew that Vincent was expected at seven. I bought two concert tickets for Reagan and left them with my friend, Linda. I told Linda I was sending Reagan over to get the tickets, and to stall her for a while because I was planning a surprise for Reagan at home.

When Reagan got home from volleyball practice, I told her about the tickets, and she eagerly set off to get them. I promised her I would entertain Vincent, and Reagan seemed glad that we would have the chance to know each other better.

At seven, Vincent arrived—not late as usual, much to my relief. I had the den of seduction all set with jasmine scented candlelight, soft jazz on the stereo, and a fresh pitcher of Watermelon Martinis poured. I put on a tight, low-cut blouse and my most seductive slacks, and I set up the tape recorder.

"Why, Vincent, you're right on time. Reagan isn't here, right now. She had an errand to run. But I would love to entertain you until she gets back."

Vincent looked very flattered, and I could tell by his leering look that he approved of my outfit. As I got closer to Vincent, I smelled the distinctive fragrance of Waterfall cologne. He took a seat next to me, and I poured him a drink, handing it to him.

"This is the kind of treatment I like: a fine woman waiting on a tired man," Vincent muttered.

"Vincent, you look very handsome, tonight. Isn't that a new leather jacket?"

"Yes, it is. I do manage to make a few bucks with a little business on the side. In fact, it is paying so well, it may just keep me in some decent threads. I might even have a little left over, too."

I moved closer to Vincent and began to massage his shoulder. I could feel his young, hard muscles pulsate under his shirt. Part of me was sickened to touch such an unsavory person, but another part responded to all the man I felt beneath my hand.

"Hey, that's nice, Bibi. You really know how to treat a man. Girls like Reagan just haven't lived long enough to know about taking care of their guys. I've always been partial to older women, anyway. Sometimes, I wonder why I'm wasting my time and energy on a child who talks about volleyball all the time!"

I loved it! I was recording all of these insults as Vincent spoke. He was digging his own grave!

"Oh, Vincent. I'm glad you appreciate older women. I sure appreciate young studs like you."

"Hey, baby, what do you say we get serious here? I know that Reagan will be coming back any minute, so let's get together at my place tomorrow night. I can do some things that only that only an older woman could appreciate. I'll rock your world, honey, and we'll leave the rest of the world in the dust! Reagan has refused my offers anyway, so why not let someone else have a chance? I've got some good weed that'll get your head right!"

At that point, I was sickened and also absolutely delighted to hear that Reagan had not succumbed to his advances. I jumped up, pretending to act thrilled about the invitation.

"Will I be the only woman in your life if I come tomorrow night? I have a feeling that Reagan is not the only girl in your life right now, and we older women are mighty jealous!"

"You're right, Bibi. I do have other women in my life, even though Reagan thinks she's the only one. But I have needs she doesn't understand like you seem to. Come over tomorrow night, and I'll guarantee you'll be the only one in my life!"

"Vincent, I think you'd better leave, now. I'll tell Reagan that you had an asthma attack and needed to go home to get your pump. You really do need to cool it with her, anyway, if we are going to get together. She doesn't understand you at all!"

"Hey, okay. You've got a deal! I'll see you at my place around eight o'clock, tomorrow night. We'll have the time of our life!" Vincent leered, as he rubbed my behind and slipped out the front door.

Shortly after, Reagan burst in, full of excitement about the concert. She looked all around, searching for lover boy.

"Honey, Vincent called and said he was ill. He'll call you tomorrow."

"Oh, poor baby! I hope he's all right! Maybe I better go over to his place!"

"No, honey. He said he had something contagious, and you don't want to get sick before the big tournament. He'll be fine."

Reagan seemed to buy the story, and after she went to her room, I rewound the tape, and I started to play it. But much to my horror, the tape was empty. Something had happened! I hadn't set the recorder properly! Now what would I do?

The next day at work, I decided that there was only one thing I could do. I would have to go over to Vincent's and tape another conversation. I hated to do it, but it was the only way. I was afraid to let any more time pass.

I lied to Reagan about where I was going, and I set off to visit Vincent that night. I had my recorder tucked safely in my purse, and I would open the purse with the recorder properly on and set when I got there.

I was shocked, when Vincent opened the door, to see the expensive furnishings in his apartment. I guess I expected a dump, but instead, I found the apartment tastefully done in a very masculine manner. Vincent had set the stage for our rendezvous, with music and liquor already flowing.

Vincent had on a cashmere sweater and tight leather pants. He wore that cologne again that really turned me on and sent my senses in a tailspin. Before I could put down my coat, Vincent grabbed me to him, and he began to kiss me.

Vincent's kisses were anything but amateurish! He kissed as

expertly as I had ever been kissed, and his young, lean body pressed hard mine. I found myself flooded with feelings I hadn't felt in years, and some I had never felt. The electricity between us was powerful enough to light up Broadway!

"Vincent, please. Let me sit down and have a drink," I begged, trying to catch my breath and regain my senses. I was there to gather incriminating evidence against him, so I had to remain clear about my mission! My recorder was running, and I would get evidence to throw that man out of our lives forever!

Vincent sat down next to me, complimenting me on my outfit. He massaged my tired shoulders. It felt so good to have strong hands touching my needy body.

I found myself closing my eyes and enjoying the feeling. Just for a moment, I told myself. It had been so long since I had been touched by any man . . . .

Again, Vincent approached me, cupping my breast in his large, strong hand.

"Bibi, you feel so good to me. Let me relax you and make you feel good, tonight. You work so hard, and you deserve a little fun in your life."

My God, I was being seduced. I knew he was just feeding me a line, but suddenly every inch of my body wanted everything he had to offer—in the worst way!

Vincent began to unbutton my blouse, carefully and expertly, not clawing at me in a way I thought a young man his age would act. Oh, he was an expert, all right. He might've been young, but he was ready. He knew exactly what he was doing.

Suddenly, I found myself nude from the waist up, with Vincent's lips on my nipples, and I began to moan ever so slightly. I had to get hold of myself! What was happening?

Carefully, Vincent guided me to his bedroom, where he pulled me onto the biggest waterbed that I had ever seen. My bare chest felt so good against the velvet bedspread, and soon Vincent's naked skin was atop mine. I didn't care about anything, anymore. I just wanted that strong, sexy man to make savage love to me!

Vincent became very passionate, and tore at my pants and underwear. He quickly ripped off the rest of his clothes, and pressed his muscular body against mine, asking me over and over again if what he was doing felt good.

All I could do was moan "yes," over and over. It was as if I were under some kind of strange spell . . . . I couldn't help but think that if he had that kind of effect on me and I had been around, my poor inexperienced daughter didn't stand a chance. Vincent was a master at his game!

Vincent made love to me three times within an hour! He brought me to higher peaks of passion than I had ever known. I felt like a woman again, and I loved how that felt.

When the novelty of what I'd done had worn off and I realized what had happened, suddenly, the weight of the world crashed down upon me. What have I just done? Haven't I learned from past experiences that being attracted to such men spells disaster?

I clearly saw my beloved Reagan's face in my mind, staring at me full of hate—and with good reason. I had betrayed her in the worst manner possible . . . sleeping with her man!

I jumped out of bed and quickly dressed. Vincent looked surprised at first, then annoyed. "Hey, baby, aren't you going to stay for more? I thought you were loving it!!!"

"Vincent, this is wrong. I can't see you, again. You are too young, and I've made a mistake. I'm afraid I'm too old for you, and my daughter is too young!"

"Bibi . . . come on! It was as good for you as it was for me. You can't walk out on me, now. We're an item; remember? You haven't seen the last of me. I didn't mean for this to happen.

I reached into my purse and destroyed the tape, throwing it in a garbage can outside of a restaurant. The only positive thing I could think of in the world was that Reagan was leaving for a week for a volleyball tournament in Dallas. At least, I had a week to decide what to do. Murder even entered my head! I might have to kill Vincent if he threatened to tell all to Reagan!

Reagan left for her tournament the next morning; she was full of smiles and excitement. I could barely look at her in the eye, but she didn't notice because she was wrapped up in her own little world.

That night, Vincent appeared at my door, all dressed up and ready for more action. I lied and said that I had company coming. I finally got him to leave, but he called me at work the following day, and he showed up again at my house. This time, I had my friend, Gerri, over, so he left without a fuss. But I knew he hadn't given up.

I guess the Lord was watching over me and I didn't know it. But I had proof the following morning when the newspaper headlines announced the largest drug bust in our city's history. Three names were published, and they were described as the masterminds behind a multi-million dollar drug ring. Vincent's name headed the top of the list. I couldn't believe my eyes!

I raced to the phone and called the police, telling them I was a friend of Vincent's. The sergeant on the phone told me I probably wouldn't lay eyes on Vincent for at least ten years this time. It came out that Vincent had a rap sheet a mile long. I couldn't believe my good fortune.

My Reagan came home to some pretty bad news, but she took it very well—especially in light of the fact that she had met a guy named Derrick at the tournament. He was also a volleyball player, and he aspired to attend the same college as she wanted. Reagan had promised him she would write to him at least once a week!

I had a very hard time forgiving myself for sleeping with Vincent—until I finally realized that I was as much of a victim of Vincent as the children he sold drugs to at the local middle school. Vincent was just one of those people who destroyed everyone in his path, but thank goodness, he didn't hurt my daughter who is on her way to a beautiful future . . . hopefully, one without any Vincent in it ever again!

THE END

SINS OF THE PAST
Led Me To A Life Lesson And A New Love!

"I'm not coming!" I shouted into the receiver. I tossed the briefcase on my new cream-colored micro fiber couch and flung myself after it. Glaring at the phone, I kicked off my shoes. "I've outgrown the country. And what is there to talk about: who got married in the church hall, and whose watermelon rind preserves tastes better? Give me a break!"

"You stuck-up little heifer! You've been in the city for two years, and all of a sudden, your family is country?" I couldn't see her, but I knew her face was torn up. That meant Gail was gathering up steam to lay me out. "You think because you went to college, moved to the city, and got some 'piece of a job,' that you're better than us?"

"Piece of a job? Let me tell you something: in case you forgot: I'm assistant director of human resources for one of the largest insurance companies in the city. And that my sister, is no piece of a job!"

"Oh yeah?" my sister spat out. "So who paid for the education to get that job? It was your countrified mother and father. You act like they asked you to move back. But don't worry, none of us could stand you every day!"

"You're just jealous!" I shouted back. "You could have gone to college, but you just had to marry Howard. It's not my fault you're just a secretary in the Board of Education, instead of having an important job like mine!"

Now, fifteen pounds and two children later, she was stuck in dinky-ass Ellisburg. She couldn't possibly be happy!

Instead of shouting, my sister let loose a low, ugly chuckle. "Jealous of you? Why? I've got a husband and children who love me. With all that big talk, I bet you don't have a man—and if you do, it's only until he finds out what a shallow little bitch you really are!"

My ear rang from the force of the phone being slammed in my ear.

It was just as well, because I had already made plans to spend Thanksgiving with my riding partners, Tina and Gloria. They were professional like me, and had long since given up the "home for the holidays" life for something more classy and elegant. We had reservations for dinner at an elegant country inn. No way would I suffer through Turkey Day with the Connors clan!

I gave my apartment an admiring glance. It was worthy of a home decorating show: cream and chocolate micro fiber furnishings, well-placed modern art—accented by a slim and elegant mirror, and a

13

custom-made coffee table embedded with sea stones. I had a service tend to the lush, dramatic houseplants that were exchanged for new varieties every three months. I was living the good life: good job, good money, good sex—who wouldn't want to be me?

But my mother had other ideas.

"Come on, honey," she pleaded. "Your daddy and I miss you. We hardly ever see you, and we're only asking for a little of your time. What's the holiday without our other baby girl?"

My mother put the guilt on me, but I fought back.

"Mom, I don't want to be surrounded by a bunch of half-drunk 'bamas waving drumsticks, ready to cuss each other out before the meal is over!"

Some of sweet pleading disappeared. "Now listen to me, Jennifer! Don't talk about your relatives like that. Don't forget where you came from. And besides, it's only a couple of hours. And by the time the game comes on, the only people getting cussed out are the two teams on the field. You know how it is."

Yeah, I did—and I wanted no parts of it. My father's side would be half-drunk, and talking loud with food in their mouths, and my mother's people would be looking like they wanted to put them all on the church's backslider list. I had suffered through enough of those when I was growing up, and swore to avoid those country-style holidays as often as I possibly could. But she wouldn't let up.

"Okay, okay!" I gave in. "I'll be there. But don't expect to see me at Christmas." I had already planned a ski-trip with the new club I'd joined. While the folks down home were drinking home-made root beer, I'd be in Colorado, sipping cognac by the fire, and looking for a fine and paid brother to hook up with.

Thanksgiving Day was worse than I thought. Every relative within fifteen miles was jammed into our three-bedroom ranch house.

"Hey baby!" my Aunt Maybelline shouted before she crushed me to her inflatable dingy chest. "Girl, you looking good! You think you could hook your old auntie up in an outfit like that?"

Dolce & Gabbana don't do hippos, I thought. The words were tempting, but high-powered executive or not, Auntie would have slapped the taste out of my mouth and left me on the floor for dead!

Disgust beamed like a beacon from my face, but it didn't keep me from being squeezed, hugged, and pinched on the cheeks by most of the people in the room. I shoved my way through the crowd of annoying relatives, and took a breather near the kitchen. Behind me, someone tapped my shoulder.

"Hi, Jennifer."

I sighed—turning to see who was left that hadn't already blasted me with a liquor-breath greeting. I was surprised to see Karlene

Brewer. She was two years younger—a shy and studious girl whose father had been our high school principal. He and my mother were peers, of sorts; she taught in the elementary school at the same time Mr. Brewer took over Ellisburg High.

"Hi, Karlene! I'm surprised to see you here. Did somebody go out and drag you in? I'm surprised there's anyone left walking the streets in this town. They all seem to be here."

Karlene giggled. "Your sharp tongue is still intact, I see." Karlene laughed. "Each year, your parents invite me and my father for Thanksgiving. You just haven't been home in a while." I felt the first twinge of guilt. Everyone must be talking about my MIA act. However, there was no judgment in her tone. She appeared to be just as sweet and good-natured as she had been during school. "There's my dad, now."

I looked around, and my mouth fell open. Back in the day, a whole lot of schoolgirls had a crush on the former football player turned educator—and with good reason. He was bona-fide fine: dark chocolate skin, broad chest, strong arms, and big feet—an attribute that wasn't lost on us. Now, Michael Brewer was drop-your-drawers gorgeous. Talk about getting better with age! Truthfully, he could stand as an equal with men half his age.

"Why, hello, Jennifer." Two deep dimples creased his jaw.

"It's been a long time since you've been home. I'm sure your parents are happy to see you."

His deep voice was like a radio announcer oozing sex at the midnight hour. Silver wings brushed the dark hair at his temples. I couldn't help but give him the once-over. Suddenly, home for the holidays was looking up—way up. So I did what any self-respecting, sexually liberated woman would do in the face of a man who looked like he could deliver: I gave him a look that oozed "open invitation." And to sweeten the deal, I touched my tongue against the center of my full and glossy top lip.

Brewer caught it. His lips turned up into a sliver of a smile.

"It was very nice to see you, Jennifer. I'm sure you've gained a lot of valuable experience living in the city."

I sure had. And if he didn't know it now, he would soon find out just how much.

Inside the dining room, I looked at my mother's handiwork. Everything—the tablecloth, napkins, serving bowls, and china, had been color-coordinated in shades of deep orange and green. I felt like I'd stumbled into a pumpkin patch. At the head of the table, she wrangled the crowd into seats. "Michael, you sit between your daughter and Jennifer. Maybelline, honey, you have to sit on the end." Some people put a hand over their mouths to hide the laughter. "Junior and Baby Boy, you two sit across from each other. I won't have any bad behavior at my table."

When she had gotten us all seated around the huge lace-covered table, my father began a blessing that turned into a "sermonette." People shifted in their chairs. When it was done, my Uncle Arnold grumbled. "Goodness, man; my head was bowed so long, I thought my neck was going to break!" And then, the passing of the food began. Potato salad crossed over string beans, hunks of ham slid by slices of turkey, and so on, until everyone's plate was full.

Halfway through the meal, Mr. Brewer leaned over. "The way you were licking your lips at me, I thought I had something you wanted to suck."

My eyes bucked. I choked hard on the biscuit that stuck halfway down my throat. Around the table, forks were halted in mid-air. To make matters worse—to anyone looking, the man's smiling face and conversational tone was directly opposite to the sexy words he whispered in my ear. When my eyes began to water, he pounded gently on my back and offered me a glass of tea.

"Honey, are you all right?" My mother rose halfway from her chair, but Mr. Brewer held up his hand. "I think the worst is over, now. Something just slid down her throat the wrong way."

I near choked again. What a choice of words! However, I didn't want to raise any more alarms. "I'm okay," I stammered, and gulped down a huge swallow of sweet tea.

I couldn't look at him. My face burned. So much for my sexy come-on. One thing was for sure. Michael Brewer was more than up for the challenge he had seen in my eyes. I could write a book about the men who thought they could get the best of me in bed—only to be reduced to begging like the homeless on the street for another taste of my sweetness.

Near the end of the meal, my mother stood again, and clapped her hands. "All right, you all; I hope you have room because it's time for dessert."

"Looking forward to it!" Brewer spoke up and smiled. "My taste buds are ready for something sweet." Before I could lift the napkin to my lips, his hand slid between my thighs. His finger made a quick, sensuous circle across the bud nestled in the crotch of my panties.

"Oh!"

I jerked against the back of my chair. It was so quick, but it felt so good, I wanted to open my legs and let him finish the job. By now, everyone was staring. Before my mother could get to me, Brewer was behind my chair.

"Let me take her into the kitchen, and see what I can do. That way, she won't get sick at the table. Remember at school, I had ad emergencies like this everyday."

Who was going to question him? He slipped his arm around my shoulder, and led me down the hall to the kitchen. A few minutes later, I heard my mother bustling down the hall to the kitchen. Thank goodness, it was a long hall. It gave Brewer just enough time to throw down the gauntlet. "I know exactly what you want, and I can give it to you. In spades. But you have to ask me nice."

I had regained some of my composure. and a lot of my boldness. I looked him up and down.

"So you think you can handle me?"

"Baby, I know your cat has claws, but my big dog will make her purr all night." The words rolled out in a conversational tone, so smooth and polished, they shocked my mouth shut. But that wasn't all. He reached behind me and palmed my breasts, pinching each nipple with just enough tortuous pressure to make them stand on end. "Oh," the moan crept out of my mouth.

By the time my mother got to the kitchen, he was leaning against the counter, cool as a cucumber. After that conversation, I expected him to be as hard as a rock, but instead, he stood there like a choirboy. "Don't worry, I've got it all under control."

"His lazy smile infuriated and inflamed me. "I used the Heimlich maneuver. If she was going to spit something out, I didn't want it to happen at the table."

Heimlich maneuver? That man was feeling me up—big time!

"Thank you Michael," my mother beamed. "I'm sure glad you knew what to do. I would have been useless, banging on her back."

"Well, sometimes banging is good. It just depends on the situation."

Oh no, he didn't! Every word out of his mouth was laden with sexual innuendos. Had a man finally turned the tables on me? And one twenty years older, at that? Right then, I decided to change my plans. If Michael Brewer thought he'd have the last word—if he were challenging me to a bedroom duel, then it was on!

The first part of my plan came together, Monday morning. I called in to work, and told them I needed a few extra days to "take care of some unexpected business."

"You're staying longer?" my mother exclaimed. "I don't know what changed your mind, but I sure am glad."

My sister—who was still on leave for an extended Thanksgiving break—turned up her nose. "Humph! You must be up to something because as I understood it, we were all too country for you."

"At least I've got something to be up to," I retorted as I breezed out of the door and headed to the center of town.

When Michael retired from teaching, he went back to his athletic roots, and opened a small fitness facility in the small downtown area. That day, I decided to sign up for a daily membership. When I pushed open the door, I had to pull my eyes back in my head. Instead of the dress shirt and slacks I'd always seen him wear, that day he wore a pair of black knee-length running shorts, and a matching short-sleeved T-shirt. The shirt sleeve capped the bulging muscles in his forearms. It lay across his broad chest. His legs were long columns of muscles under the black knee-length running shorts. Sexy and classy were the best words to describe him that morning.

I waved my hand around the gym. The space was small, but neat with state of the art equipment, an offering of T-shirts with the gym's logo stitched on the pockets, and a small juice bar. "So what else do you have to offer?" I purred like a kitten aching to be stroked.

His eyebrow rose. "You mean you came to see if this small-town gym could complete with what you're used to?" His gaze raked me from head to toe. "Or something else?"

This man sure knew how to run a game. I wondered who else he was playing with, and if she could keep up? One thing was certain: I'd bet no woman his age could give him what he needed. It took a woman like me—with serious bedroom skills and a body that brought men to their knees. I smoothed my hand over the skirt so tight, it could have been painted over my curves. "It depends on what you've got."

Michael leaned up from the long counter.

"Come on into my office and fill out an application for temporary membership. Then, I'll give you the tour."

The place between my thighs was already quivering in anticipation of "the tour." We'd take each other around the world and back again—right there in his office. And that would make it more exciting, knowing that there were people sweating outside while we were making each other wet just a door away. . .

He closed the door behind us and leaned against his desk.

"I remember you from school. You were one of those center-of-attention girls—fine and you knew it. Only the strong could survive with you. Your hips swayed side to side like a stripper turned runway model."

Before he could continue, I crossed my legs. My short skirt rode up, giving him a view of my long butter-smooth legs ending in ankle-strapped, three-inch heels. I uncrossed them, leaned back in the chair, and spread my legs wide open. The panties I wore barely covered my "good girl," and I let him have the wide-angled view.

His lids dropped; a smile pulled at one corner of his mouth that I knew was good for all kinds of pleasure. Brewer crossed his muscular arms, and gave my offering a long, stare. I knew I had him, then—

18

until he grabbed my hand and pressed it between his legs. I felt him surge against my palm. He kept his hand over mine, and guided it up and down over his bone-hard erection. "Show me yours, I'll show you mine."

Just as quickly, he dropped my hand and turned to the papers on his desk.

"Now, are you ready for that tour?"

"Tour!" I gasped. "Tour of what?" I thought, by now, he'd have me spread-eagled on the desk, or at least have his hand underneath my panties. In fact, it was what I was aching for—every time I thought about that little under-the-table appetizer, I was primed and ready.

"I thought that's why you came: to sign up for a temporary membership while you're here—especially since I hear you decided to stay a few more days. Can't let those Thanksgiving calories ruin that tight body, now can you? And by the way, I don't like being interrupted. You didn't let me finish, so I'll do it now. As I was saying, I wasn't then, and I am not now, a fool. As much as I would have liked to tame your fine ass and give you the ride of your life, my job was more important than my johnson. I don't play with underage girls. Even if you were legal, you were too stuck on yourself. And from what I can see, you still are."

I shot up from the chair. "Wait a minute! Who—"

Michael cut me off, smiled broadly and patted me on the arm. "Temper, temper," he drawled. "Not good for the blood pressure, you know."

What in the hell was his problem? And why was he stringing me along and insulting me? As fine as I was, offering him the best sex of his life on a silver platter, and he was playing cat and mouse, or cat and dog. From what I had felt, he was definitely right about his big dog. And in spite of the fact that he put me in my place, I wanted it to bite me even more!

That night, I called my friend, Gloria. I was bursting to tell somebody about what was happening. I sprawled out on the bed in my old room and pulled out the yearbook. There was Mr. Brewer looking like the consummate professional, instead of the freak he turned out to be. "Girl, you won't believe it! My old high school principal was here for dinner. And Lord, he's even finer than he was in high school. We used to fantasize about him, wondering if his feet were any indication of the length of his pipe!"

"Oooh, Gloria exclaimed. "So I know you took care of that and had him begging for more. An older man, huh? I hope you didn't kill him?"

I didn't want to admit it, but Gloria had been my best friend since we met in the hair salon, and I could tell her anything. "It's the other way around," I mumbled.

"What! You mean the woman we call 'The Slayer' has met her match? And with an old dude, at that? You know you've got to give me all the details on this one!"

I filled her in on the game Brewer was playing with me, and how he had me chasing him down. "He might be old, but girl, he is fine and fit! When I walked into that gym and saw his muscles in those legs, I tried to give him some on the spot. But he acted like he was a celibate priest—except when he made me feel his thang."

"Did it match his feet? But wait a minute—that's all? Oh girl, I know you're not used to that. So what are you going to do?"

"I'm going to become his daughter's new best friend."

In warp speed, I resurrected my acquaintance with Karlene. We went to the movies, had lunch, and had even planned some Black Friday shopping.

That evening, I brought a bottle of wine and finger food for a night of movies and an overnight stay at her house. We were seated in front of the big-screen TV in their basement, catching up on each other's lives. "So how do you like the city?" she asked.

"Oh, I love it; there's always something to do, something to see, and lots of interesting people to see it with. I don't think I could ever live anywhere else. How about you? Why did you come back after college?"

I curbed my judgmental urge to ask her why in the hell anybody would come back to this country-ass backwater town, but it would defeat my purpose to get in her good graces and closer to her father. I know I could have busted through the door wearing nothing but a trench coat, but this elaborate game of seduction was infinitely more sexy and arousing.

My nipples tightened when I heard the heavy thud of footsteps on the basement steps. Michael poked his head around the door. "Just checking in on you two. I'm going back to the gym to take care of some paperwork."

I took his announcement as an invitation. I could hardly wait.

When Karlene fell asleep, I changed from my plain girl's night out pajamas into a candy pink man-pleaser. The back of my thong was a mere piece of dental floss covering the line between my cheeks. The tight-ribbed top ended five inches above my belly button and fit tight against my voluptuous breasts—highlighting my slender waist and the flat belly I worked hard to maintain.

I threw on a coat and shoes and crept outside. When I pulled into the parking lot, I knew the door was unlocked for me. I pushed it open and found Michael in his office, sitting on the couch with his arms crossed behind his head. He blinked slowly, treating himself to a full view of my sexy beauty.

"Nice," he murmured. "I see you came dressed for the occasion."

I twirled around, giving him a good view of what was in store for him.

"I'm about to give you the ride of your life," I smirked.

"Still got a quick tongue," he chuckled. "Let me see just how talented it is."

Before I wondered what he was packing below the belt, and now that I was face-to-face with that magnificent specimen, my eyes grew wide. But I was up to the task. I took him in slowly. He began to groan, a low, guttural, primal sound. When his hips pumped, thrusting until he touched the back of my throat, I knew I was doing my job, and doing it well. I stopped, and pulled back to tease him. Michael grabbed handfuls of my hair and held me in place while my lips and tongue blasted him to paradise. He sank back, throwing both arms above his head, against the pillow. "Nice," he murmured.

"Nice!" I exploded. "I just blew your brains out, and all you can say is nice? I've been with men who have offered me cars, cash, jewelry, and trips around the world after one taste of this!" I pointed to my crotch. "So I don't know what your problem is!"

He regarded me with that same lazy look. "You talk too much. And your ego is as big as your mouth. Now, shut up and let me school you."

And that's exactly what my former principal did. That man did things with his mouth and tongue that I never imagined possible. And I thought I had experienced it all. There was no emotional pretense: no hugging, no kissing, just getting down to business with pure, hard-driving, no-holds-barred sex. The self-control I vowed to exhibit was nonexistent. When his fingers stroked between my legs, my body rose so high off the couch, I imagined myself suspended in space. He flipped me over. My hands clawed the leather as he drove deep inside me, slaying me with each long stroke. Just before I burst into a thousand pieces, he turned me on my back, hooked his arms under my knees, and opened me wide for the grand finale. I cried, whimpered, and begged while he teased—until he drove in with one last masterful thrust that left me dead on the battlefield of unimagined pleasure.

The time for fronting was over. I had been completely dominated by a man I derisively referred to as "the old dude." From my place on the sofa bed, I looked over at him.

He was already sitting up. "Now that I've made my point and we've had our fun, I'm going to take a shower. You need to take one yourself, and go on home. I'll tell Karlene you had to leave early."

I sat up, pulling the sheet over me—although it was ludicrous—since he'd been in almost every cavity of my body.

"Why are you doing this? You treat me like a discarded piece of tissue when you wanted me as much as I wanted you!"

He turned his head to stare at me.

"Ah, you don't like it when the tables are turned, huh? Always want to be in control, calling the shots and treating everybody else like trash—in bed and out?"

"What makes you think you can talk to me like that?" I raged.

"Because I can," he told me in a soft voice that brooked no nonsense. "You blew into town like you were doing everybody a favor—especially your family. What you don't know is that your brother-in-law and I are very good friends. He was upset when he told me the things you'd said to your sister, calling your family country, bragging about your men, your job, and your possessions. So when you gave me that look, I knew two things: You were arrogant enough to believe you could beat me in bed, and that I was going to teach you a lesson. And now that my work is over, I'm finished!"

I slunk home like a bragging prizefighter who'd been knocked out in the first round. For the rest of the night, I stayed awake, reviewing my life, the choices I'd made, and the reasons I needed to prove myself at the expense of others.

When I got up the next morning, my mother was at the counter, measuring coffee for our breakfast.

"Here, let me help you. I might be a boss in the office, but I'm still your daughter at home."

"Jennifer!" My mother cried out and pulled me into her fragrant warmth. "Oh, baby, that is sweet music to my ears. I've been praying for the day when you would come back to us—in every way."

It was because of Michael Brewer, although I didn't dare tell her how he'd made me realize the error of my ways. He took the same weapon I'd used and turned it back onto me. In the process, he made me jump off that ivory tower where I had placed myself. He made me recognize how utterly shallow I had been, belittling my family and lording my position and possessions over anybody who would listen. It was strange—despite how he taught me that lesson, my admiration for his character surpassed that of his physical ability. And for a woman like me, that was saying a lot! There was one more thing I had to admit to myself: he was the kind of man I really wanted—but could I ever find my way into his good graces and make our sexual collision an affair of the heart as well? I was determined to try. All he could say was no.

"You might as well get ready to see me at Christmas, too." I promised. And I meant it. My family would love me if I had a thrift store couch and hand-me-down clothes. So it was time to return that love in all the ways that mattered.

THE END

22

SAVING MY
LITTLE SISTER
Forced Me Into The Netherworld
Of Thugs And Hip-Hop

I never thought I would be crawling into the seedy underbelly of the hip-hop world because of my missing sister. For as long as I could remember, all she cared about was the music and rap artists on television that made the thug life seem like it was an exciting way to live.

Music TV and the newer stations touted rump-shaking young girls exhibiting as much of their sexual attributes as prime time censorship would let them get away with.

It seemed that ever since rap made its debut, everybody and his sorry ass singer wanted to be a rap artist. Little did they know or seem to care that the real money was in producing, songwriting, and promoting. In the eyes of the young, if it wasn't right in your face, then it didn't exist. All the young bloods wanted was to perform in a club, a stadium, or on TV as soon as they possibly could. Only a few had real talent; the rest of them were mimicking the all-readys and the has-beens.

I can remember chastising Tiffany for spending so much time in front of the television watching the sexy videos.

"Girl, if you knew your history as well as you know that music, you'd be passing your tests." I chided.

"And if you had any business, you'd be minding it!" She snapped back.

She never used to talk to me or anyone that way; she used to have respect. If she were here now, instead of out there with Jovay, I would let her watch as much hip-hop as she wanted.

Jovay a.k.a. Joey Vega was a small time hood rat with aspirations of being the next big thing in music. A local club let him perform, and they weren't particular about who they let in. If you looked eighteen, then you were eighteen—even when the fake ID was as obvious as a mole on a witch's chin. I'd heard that girls flocked to his shows like bees to honey—and my sister was no exception.

If my parents knew what I was about to do, they would freak and lock me up before they would allow me to do it! But my mother was grief-stricken because Tiffany—her baby—had been missing for two weeks.

I had to find her, and becoming a hip-hop groupie, wasn't something I'd ever think I'd be doing, but it was the only way. There's a whole other seedy underworld in the hip-hop culture that the public doesn't know about. That next Saturday, I entered it.

Club Xenon was the most popular hip-hop meeting place for established and wannabe artists. Every Friday and Saturday nights, there were no less than five or six high profile celebrity artists either performing or just coming to scope out the competition.

It was almost twenty miles away, and things didn't start jumping until ten, and the party usually went on well into the wee hours of the morning—sometimes, beyond.

Dressing the part, I donned a slick short tight, skirt, a Kimora Lee fashion top, and a Baby Phat studded purse. I wasn't Missy Elliot, but I looked liked I belonged.

Xenon was bustling with people from the world of hip-hop music and their cohorts. Everybody had a big burly bodyguard that looked liked he could take down an army of Sumo wrestlers single-handedly. The women were of all colors, with each trying to outdo the other with their clothes and ostentatious hairstyles. It was like watching a game unfold with everybody vying for the win. I was appalled to see so many girls whom I was sure was underage with stars in their eyes, hoping to be chosen out by one of the visiting musical royalty.

I had no trouble getting in. All I needed was attitude and twenty-five dollars. Once inside, I wasn't surprised to see several white men dressed in the urban styles of the culture that they shunned by day, but sneaked around in at night. In order to belong, they talked like us, walked like us, but didn't ever want to wake up in our skin.

The place was a huge refurbished warehouse, with corners and nooks filled with groups of people doing things I didn't want to think about Tiffany ever being involved in.

As I moved into bar area, I passed an alcove where a girl that couldn't have been more than sixteen, giving a lap dance to a man who had obviously exposed himself to her undulating bottom.

I bit my tongue as hands rubbed along the curve of my behind or touched my breasts. Men rubbed their hard members against me, and when I looked at them with anger, they merely licked their lips—offering a suggestion of how they could pleasure me orally.

Luckily, I found a seat at the far end of the long horseshoe shaped bar, but it was impossible to get the attention of any of the busy bartenders.

"Can I buy you a drink?"

I looked up at the man who had made the offer. He was tall and thin. His pants hung low on his waist, exposing his stripped underwear. His brogan shoes were suede with gold colored laces, and his bald head was covered with a baseball cap that was turned around backwards.

"Thanks, I can buy my own." I said dismissing him.

Besides, I'd heard about how certain drugs were put into drinks, and women could barely remember the degrading things that might have happened to them, later.

"That's not very friendly." He smiled, crookedly exposing a front tooth that had a quarter carat diamond pasted on it.

He wasn't a man used to being denied or ignored, and I shivered a little when his eyes turned cold, but the smile was still there.

"Suit yourself; there's plenty of other hos."

He turned and walked into the sea of undulating bodies on the dance floor.

Someone squeezed by me, tapping the mahogany bar and waving a fifty-dollar bill. The gold lion's head pinky ring had two brilliant diamonds for eyes, and glinted magnificently even in the dim light of the bar area.

"Yo, BeZee! Lemme have a Dewer's neat."

The bartender nodded, and proceeded to fill the order.

"You must have some clout in here. I've been waiting fifteen minutes; they've been ignoring me like I was yesterday's news."

He barely glanced at me, but took his drink, and sipped it when the bartender set it in front of him.

"Thanks, BeZee. And hey, give the lady what she wants. Keep the change."

I was about to explain that I didn't want him to buy me a drink, but all I could see was his back as he walked away in the slickest, most neatly tailored and obviously expensive black suit I'd ever seen.

"What'll you have?"

"Merlot." I answered, "but I'd rather pay for my own drink."

"Suit yourself."

The bartender shrugged, and went off to prepare it.

I surveyed the room, hoping to catch a glimpse of Jovay, but it was impossible in the sea of bodies that moved like a dark wave on the ocean.

I took a small sip of wine. I wasn't a drinker, but I had to at least appear to be part of the scene. I needed to circulate and search for Tiffany, so I took my drink and wove my way though the throng of dancers. The music was loud, and people were really spellbound with it, liquor, and I'm sure—drugs.

Girls were doing the most decadent dance moves, grinding their pelvis' against he distended crotches of men just standing there accepting their favor. One young woman was sandwiched between two men, her skirt pulled high, and I could see she wore no underwear! One of the men slipped his hand between her legs, then brought it back out, and forced it between her lips—which she suckled

25

erotically. Another woman sat on the lap of a man, whom I thought I recognized as a singer from UH1-Soulvision, and she was obviously performing a sex act right out in the open!

Disgusted, I turned away. A young woman slammed into me, causing the wine to splatter on both of us.

"What the hell is yo problem, bee-otch?" she slurred, looking me up and down.

"I'm sorry, I didn't mean—"

"You're sorry, all right—a sorry ass. Look at my top. I just got it off layaway, and you done ruined it."

"I'm sure a little seltzer water will get that right out."

I tried to explain.

"Stupid heifer . . . get the hell outta my face."

I moved around the girl, and headed for the ladies room—hoping to dab at the stain on my own top.

It was a unisex bathroom, with men and women standing around, talking, smoking weed, or groping one another. A tall man stood near the stalls with a woman who was on her knees with a dog's choker collar around her neck.

"One dollar, and she'll clean you good when you're done in there," he said, yanking at the collar, and nodding to the stall.

I wanted to throw up. My sister would never be part of this lifestyle—even she had to see that. I knew I had to start asking questions to find out if anyone knew where she was.

As I entered the stall, I was suddenly pushed in from behind. My heart raced as I felt myself being shoved over the dirty toilet.

"You make one sound, and I'll cut your throat."

I fought to keep from passing out as my body shook with fright.

"When a man offers you a drink, you should be more polite."

I felt him pressing himself up against my panties, and I struggled to free myself.

"This is what all you hos come here for: A little fun and a lot of release."

His hand moved over my mound, and I squeezed my legs together tightly.

"Ooh girl . . . . yeah, that's it; work them muscles. Is that what you're like on the inside?"

His hand moved to the waistband of my panties, and I knew I was in serious trouble.

"Maybe I'll call some of my boys, and we can run a train on you. A snooty booty like you can stand to be taken down a peg."

I was scared to death. I began to kick backwards, but he held me fast. Just as he was about to snatch my panties down, I felt air as someone snatched him off me.

26

"You getting ready to push up on my woman, Lover Man?"

The voice was unmistakable. It was the Dewer's man from the bar.

"Whoa, Salique, I didn't know she was your ho. You need to put some signs on your ladies, man. How a brotha gonna know?"

"All a brotha needs to do is ask."

I turned in time to see the one called Lover Man make a hasty retreat.

Sighing with relief, I was about to thank my savior, when he grabbed my arm, and pulled me from the stall. Draping his arm possessively around me, he walked me out of the bathroom.

"Just keep walkin'," he whispered in my ear.

What had I gotten myself into? Was he going to finish what Lover Man had started? I tensed, my eyes searching for an avenue of escape. He held me tighter, moving me toward the exit.

Cool air caressed my face as he walked passed the bouncer at the door.

"Have a nice evening, Salique," the man said, lasciviously.

He ignored the bouncer as he urged me toward a gleaming black Jaguar parked nearby.

"Get in!" he growled.

"Look. . . ."

He opened the door, and pressed against me.

"Get in," his voice was an ominous whisper.

I slid into the seat, my mind already trying to devise a way to get out of this new situation.

He got in, started the engine, and took off down the street.

It was late, and there wasn't much traffic. He came to an abrupt halt in the darkness of the entrance of Lockland Park. I knew this was it: this was where he would rape me—or worse, leaving my lifeless body by the side of the road.

He turned to me, and even in the low light, I could see the hard handsomeness of his face.

"Just what the hell did you think you were doing? Slumming for the night?"

"Excuse me?" I asked, perplexed.

"You've never been in that kind of club in your life. Don't you know what goes on in there?"

"What makes you so sure?"

"Are you kidding; you stuck out like a cotton ball on a pile of coal. Why do you think Lover Man went after you?"

"Because he's slime."

"He's a sexual predator. Although, I must admit you're a little older than his usual prey."

I was incensed at the insult.

"And who do you think you are? Ice-T from Criminal Intent? And what kind of name is Salique, anyway? It sounds like a Dollar Store joke!"

"Where do you live? I'm taking you home, and I'd better not ever see you at Xenon, again." he said, ignoring my insulting his name.

"I have to go back."

"Why? To get yourself raped or killed?" He yelled.

"I've got to find my baby sister, she's only sixteen. I think she might be with some creep named Jovay."

"Joey Vega?" He whistled lightly. "He's a bad dude. How the hell did she get mixed up with him?"

"I found a card in her room. He was looking for girls to be in his video. His number was on the back."

"I haven't seen Joey for more than two weeks." He mused, rubbing his chin.

"I'm so scared something bad has happened to her. Look, you're in that world; maybe you can help me. I can give you money. It's not much, but you can have it all."

"Where do you live?" He asked, quietly.

I wasn't about to give him my address so that he could come back and harass me. I was about to tell him so when his cell phone rang. I was surprised to see him reach under his seat to retrieve it.

"Detective Young."

I was stunned. He was a cop?

After a short conversation, he snapped the phone shut.

"Now, will you let me take you home?"

On the way, he told me how he'd followed Lover Man after he saw me entering the ladies room. He said he had seen firsthand what he'd done to women in the past, and couldn't stand by while another woman was brutally assaulted. He said that he was sorry about my sister, but he was on a big undercover drug operation, and very close to making an arrest. He couldn't compromise himself by helping me. I pleaded with him, but it was no good. He left me at my door—tearful and hopeless.

The next week, I returned to Xenon. I was dressed to the nines. And this time, I acted like I belonged. I spotted Salique at the bar, a slim willowy blond leaning against him. I walked right to him, and pressed my body close—taking his tongue into my mouth like I was suck starting a Humvee. I felt his arm snake around my slim waist. Releasing his lips, I turned to the girl.

"Beat it, sister!"

The tone in my voice, and the color of my skin let her know I meant business in a place where she was outnumbered, and surely unwanted by the regular female populace.

"I told you not to come back," he whispered as he continued to hold me.

I ground myself against him as I'd seen the other women do."

Pressing my lips close, I nibbled and whispered back. "And I told you, I have to find my sister. If you don't help me, I'm sure the thugs here would love to know that five-oh is in the house."

He breathed in hard, and I felt a stirring below his belt.

"Its nothing personal. It happens when any sexy woman throws herself at me, " he said.

"I'm nothing like them, and I'm not throwing myself—"

I tried to move away, but he held me close.

"Hey, we'd better keep up appearances," he said, and kissed me again. "So, what's your name?"

"Miki," I said. "And yours?"

"It's Earl, but you better call me Salique, or better yet, how about—Baby?"

He spun me around so that I faced the crowd, but still leaned against him as his hands roamed over my hips. I was about to tell him that he was enjoying himself a little too much when I saw them. It was Tiffany, and who could only be Jovay. He was medium height, and as stocky as a bull. His shaved head had tribal tattoos over it that coiled down and around his neck. He glittered with more bling than Mr. T ever had, and he moved like a jungle cat. Tiffany didn't look happy, and I could see a small bruise below her left eye.

"That's her! That's Tiffany!" I hissed.

"Be cool." He turned me to him, once again. "Just be cool."

Just then, two burly men approached us.

"Evenin' Salique, enjoying yourself?"

"Hey, my man, Dusty; what's goin' on?"

He pounded the man's fist with a brother's handshake.

"Not much, except I heard a rumor that we may have a mole in here. This your new lady?"

The man's eyes scathed over me, and I fought not to shudder.

"You got to be kiddin' me—a cop? In here?"

"Yeah, that's what I heard. Say, I have that stuff you wanted. How about we go and have a taste." The man's feral eyes never left mine.

"Sure, Dusty; whatever you say."

He kissed me, and smacked me smartly on the butt.

"Bring your lady."

It was more an order than a request.

I followed them to the back, Earl made sure I was between the men so that I couldn't be seen by Tiffany.

Inside the plush office, there was an ornate bar with crystal glasses, a desk, and a long leather couch.

Dusty went to a wall safe, and extracted a square package. With a small sharp knife, he slit it and extracted a line of fine white powder.

"Have a snort. It's the best nose candy you'll find, anywhere!"

"Man, I was about to take my lady and get my freak on."

"Maybe she'd like some, too?"

It was clearly a challenge.

"I don't need any stimulation to please my man," I spoke up.

Dusty took the knife, and held it to his own nose, snorting up the powder. He closed his eyes as the euphoric cloud hit his brain.

"Go on, little lady. Let me see what you can do—unless, of course, you're five-oh—and in that case, can't do it."

He thought I was the undercover cop. He'd never really seen me there before, and Earl had been in deep cover for almost a year.

Never in my life had I performed a sex act in front of an audience. I looked at Earl, he smiled, but there was something behind his gaze. A pleading, but for what, I didn't know.

I did know that if we had any chance to get out of this, and get Tiffany to safety, I would have comply.

I knelt in front of Earl and unzipped his fly. I reached inside to extract him and felt the warm steel strapped to his inner leg. I pulled him free and pasted my mouth against him. He gripped my shoulders, and it was more of a gesture pushing me slightly away. I heard Dusty move to get a better view, and I went full speed ahead and took Earl into my mouth. With long, noisy slurps, I pleasured him. I knew it was too much for him.

I said nasty things in between. The men were focused on what I was doing, and I was scared to death as I reached in and unsnapped the gun. I knew Earl was close to climax. His breathing increased as a moan crawled up out of his throat. Just as he was about to burst, I yanked the gun free and spun around—waving it haphazardly. Through a drug haze, Dusty reached for his own gun, but I shut my eyes and fired. I felt myself being pushed back, and the gun snatched from my hand. I covered my ears as the barrage of gunshots filled the air.

Outside, there was pandemonium as I heard the words, "Police, everybody freeze!"

I got up, hardly noticing Dusty's bodyguard leaning against the wall, holding his hand over his belly. Dusty tried to catch his breath as blood poured from a wound in his chest.

I ran outside, screaming for Tiffany. Moments later, I heard her calling my name. Then, she was in my arms.

"I'm sorry, Mikki; I'm so sorry."

"It's okay, now. You're safe. We're going home."

Detective Earl Young cleared us through, and had an officer drive us home.

It was two weeks before he came to see me.

"I'm sorry about the delay, but there was a lot of paperwork and pre-trial hearings. How's your sister?"

I told him that Tiffany refused to talk about what had happened during her time with Joey Vega, and I had to put her in a counseling program.

I was embarrassed, but I felt I needed to tell him why I did what I did. He held up his hand to stop me.

"Look I want to apologize for putting you in that position. There's nothing I can say to make up for it."

It was water under the bridge, and neither of us could do anything about it.

"But maybe dinner might be a start," he offered.

"I'd like that," I said, smiling. "But after what I did for you, it had better be some dinner!"

His laughter filled the air, and I knew it was the start of a very special relationship.

THE END

LOVE LESSONS
In My Student's Arms… Not Even
Being Fired Mattered!

I was hard pressed to keep my mind on my work whenever I remembered the way Miles' eyes bore into mine and he touched my hand when he helped me pick up my fallen papers earlier that day. My stomach knotted with delight every time I thought about his chestnut brown bedroom eyes. There was something lazily seductive about them—as well in his sexy smile that sent shivers up my spine.

Suddenly, shame filled my whole being. Miles Chandler was my underage student. He wasn't exactly jailbait, but it wouldn't look right that his older teacher macked on him. It would be more easily understood and accepted if a student had a crush on his teacher, than for the opposite to be true. No one would condone my having the hots for Miles. I tried to tell myself that that wasn't the case, but since the first day he walked into my history class and smiled at me, I'd felt an undeniable attraction to him.

He was built like an older man: tall, bulging muscles, and well proportioned in every way. And he was packing—if you know what I mean. To be blunt, the brother had the body of life. Talk about handsome: Miles was beyond fine. He was manly, but he also had a gentle way about him as well as a voice so bass-filled, that I was sure that only the wilds of nature could hear it. He was a loner and didn't seem very comfortable with his classmates. He also had an obvious crush on me—which didn't help matters one bit.

I found myself daydreaming about being locked in his embrace around the clock—and that wasn't a good thing. Instinctively, I knew that I was treading into dangerous territory, but my heart would let me feel anything else but longing for him.

Everyday, I looked forward to seeing Miles saunter into my English class, and he'd stop to give me his sweet, sexy smile. Without fail, he always hung around after class after the other students left and asked me if there was anything he could do for me. I always declined his offers—hoping that he couldn't tell how attracted I was to him and how much I was ready to do wild things to him.

My breath quickened, and my face warmed because I was sure he could rock my world. That afternoon I dropped my papers, was the first time Miles ever actually touched me. Even though it was just to grasp my hand, my body felt as if sinew were on fire. As we stopped to retrieve the papers, our gazes caught and held, and it told me things no young man his age should know!

"What's your first name, Ms. Lindsay?" His voice was intimate and sensuous; his manner confident and mesmerizing—as if he could read everything I felt.

"It's Sherry. Why do you want to know?" I rubbed my thighs together, unable to hide my discomfort at his closeness.

Miles smiled and held my hand, gently squeezing it as he helped me to my feet. Then, he handed me my spilled papers.

"Sherry. That's pretty; it sounds like a fine wine that gets better with age. I figured your name would be as pretty as you." A wide smile overtook his features, disarming me. I returned it, basking in the delightful smell of his Hummer cologne.

"May I help you with anything, Sherry? He asked, saying my name in an almost musical tone. The way he said it sent shivers of desire up my spine.

"I can carry those things for you," Miles said, making his usual offer.

I shook my head, backing away. I didn't trust myself to speak—feeling that he'd pick up on the heat laced in my words. To be honest, the sight of that young man set my loins ablaze.

He stared at me, letting his eyes linger for longer than they should have. Then, they scanned my body from head to toe and they swept back to my face.

My heart thudded like a bass drum and my pulse raced under the scrutiny of his gaze. I hoped that he was pleased by what he saw. Something inside of me was sure that he was.

Heat filled my face. How can I let myself feel like this about my student? I don't want him to think I'm just a horny teacher who can't get any! I thought.

"Uh, excuse me, Miles. I'm late for a staff meeting," I whispered, hurrying out of the room.

"Get yourself together, girlfriend," I scolded myself as I headed to the Teacher's Lounge. The thoughts I was having about Miles were totally off the chain. I was a teacher, and he was a student looking for English instruction, not in the ways of love! I couldn't allow myself to lose sight of my purpose for being at the Sojourner Truth Learning Center of Creative Arts. It was to teach the students—not to romance them. Yet, I couldn't stop thinking about Miles and wondering what it would be like to be wrapped up tight in his muscular arms and kissing him senseless.

My body stayed on fire most of the time as I imagined myself making love with him—a man-child nearly a decade my junior. I had to stop thinking about him in that way. It could only lead to trouble for both of us, I decided.

At the end of the school week, I was tired—both physically and emotionally. I was happy that it was finally Friday, and I was relieved to be getting away from Miles for a couple of days. I was also already regretting the time that I wouldn't be able to see him.

I shopped for groceries for my dinner and I hurried home. I had test papers from several classes to grade, lesson plans to make for the next week, reports to write, and handouts and materials to create— busy work that would help keep my mind occupied and off Miles for most of the weekend, I tried to convince myself.

After a rare home-cooked dinner, I did the monstrous paperwork that lay before me—breaking occasionally to relax or to grab something to snack on. I was knee deep in grading papers and making comments to the students about their errors, when I came across Miles Chandler's paper.

My first reaction was to smile—surprised and pleased that I had worked my way into those test papers already. I opened the folder and glanced at some of his answers, thinking that he was one of the best students in any of my classes. My eyes got big and round when I looked closely at the message he'd written at the bottom of the paper.

I can't get you out of my mind, Sherry. Please let me love you.

Fondly,

Miles

I couldn't stop reading it. My heart nearly pounded out of my chest. I smiled slowly as I thought about the message and its author— then I closed my eyes and hugged his paper to my bosom. I thought about how wonderful it would feel to let Miles love me. There was nothing that would give me greater pleasure.

I opened my eyes again, and I stared at the message, frowning. Now what? How am I supposed to treat this? What does Miles expect me to do? I thought.

"Oh, Miles. Why did you write this? This complicates things more than you'll ever know. It's crazy," I whispered as a rush of heat washed over me—even then. I longed for Miles to love me, and that I could return his feelings—but it couldn't happen. I cringed as I imagined the horrible fate that would befall me if anyone knew that I was even thinking about him in any other way than a student.

"I wish I could love you back, Miles," I whispered, placing a soft kiss on his paper. With great trepidation, I set it aside.

I tried to finish my paperwork, but I couldn't concentrate another minute. All I could think of was Miles and how much I wanted to be with him, how crazy it all was, and what could be the result of my acting on my forbidden cravings.

Finally, I stopped faking the funk, and I went to bed. I tossed and turned, imagining that Miles was making mad passionate love to me on some faraway, exotic island. My body was tortured and on fire. My mind tried desperately to block those feelings. There was no answer. I told myself over and over that I had to stop thinking about Miles in that way, but my heart and body protested. Fatigue finally lulled me into a fitful sleep in which I dreamed again about making love with Miles.

In the dream, our lovemaking was getting to the point of no return, but just as I was about to climax, bells began to go off all around us. Somehow, we were in my classroom. The bright lights glared, and people stood around, pointing fingers of shame at us—shaking their heads in disgust. I tried to make Miles get up off me, but he held onto me tightly, looking at me with eyes of love as if he didn't see anyone else.

"I knew this would happen," I said over and over as if the words would change the situation. But deep inside, I only wished the bells would stop ringing. The shrill sound became louder and louder as I wrestled to wake up. Finally, I sprang bolt upright in my bed, my eyes flying open in panic. I still heard the bells very clearly as I wiped the perspiration from my face. I had a panic attack as I hyperventilated to the point that breathing into a paper bag didn't help me.

A moment later, I frowned, realizing that the bells I heard were real: it was my doorbell. I turned on the lamp and looked at the clock. It was after two a.m. I wondered who in their right mind would be at my door that ungodly hour. I figured that something must've been wrong, so I pulled on my robe and answered the door. I was shocked to see Miles standing on my porch, his hands jammed into his pockets. White heat permeated my loins at the sight of him looking so sexy in the moonlight.

"Miles? What are you doing here?" I quizzed, hoping he'd have a good enough excuse that I could invite him in.

Stark fear glittered in his eyes, and he looked about as nervous as a ho in church. He kicked at the porch railing, stepping closer to the door.

"I woke you up. I'm sorry, Sherry. . . I uh, need to talk to you. May I come in?" His hand reached for the door.

"How did you get my address?" I asked, stalling to quell the feeling of fear that engulfed me.

"You're listed in the phone book. That's why I wanted to know your first name."

I nodded, my mind burning with remembrance of the day he asked me. I wasn't sure if I should let him come in. I was afraid of myself and of what I might do to him if he were near me outside of a school setting. He must have sensed my reticence. His eyes pleaded with me, sending a message that only we understood.

"Sherry? Please. I'm going crazy," he whispered, his voice sounding miserable.

I hesitated only a moment longer, sucked in a deep breath, and I inched the door open. I stepped inside to let him in. My robe accidentally popped open, revealing my satin nightgown. I closed it quickly before he saw what he didn't need to see.

"Okay, Miles. But only for a few minutes," I said with futility, knowing in my heart that I was asking for the very trouble I had been avoiding since he walked into my classroom at the beginning of the semester. I pushed the door and locked it, not bothering to turn on the light. I knew what was bothering him, what he wanted when he called me by my first name. It was the same thing that had tormented me night and day.

"What is it, Miles?" I could see his handsome face in the moonlit darkness as he stepped close to me.

Trouble—big trouble, my inner voice screamed.

"I love you, Sherry. I can't stop thinking about you. I'm going crazy. I know I'm just a kid—" He sighed and stepped even closer to me, his eyes begging me to understand. "Sherry?"

He pulled me into the circle of his arms, and I felt myself trembling as my body pressed close to his. He didn't have to say anything else. There was no sense pretending. My arms held him even closer, and we kissed until we were breathless. Without words, I led him to my bedroom—eager to feel his naked body pressed close to mine.

He undressed us quickly, leaving a trail of clothes where we'd trod. As we lay in bed, I let my hands explore his hard, muscular body—shamelessly reveling in pleasure of the readiness of his eager manhood. He kept whispering that he loved me, his hands caressing and massaging my breasts, my stomach, my hips, then the hungry mound he yearned for.

I shivered with pleasure, my body aching for the fulfillment I had fantasized about for so long. Miles moaned like a starving man who had finally been given food. Each time he did, I thought my own heart would burst. I had never felt so much emotion and desire like I did at that moment.

"Miles," I whispered, my voice husky with lust and longing as I pleasured him. He climbed atop me and joined us as one. He began stroking, but the rhythm was a bit too hard and too fast.

"Slow down, Miles," I whispered, placing my hands on his hips to tamp down his movements. I could tell that he would explode too soon if I didn't reel him in.

He kicked his movements down a notch, and he even stopped several times when I pressed my hands around his buttocks to signal that I wasn't ready.

Finally, I kissed him and moaned, moving my hips to meet his thrusts. I felt him convulse inside me, then he began to whimper. I tightened my arms around him as my own body demanded its release. Together, our moans meshed into one long, continuous moan—joining us as one body, one flesh.

Entwined in each other's arms, Miles relaxed and lay on me. "You're so precious and beautiful, Sherry. I love you! Please love me back," he whispered, stroking his face against mine.

"I do love you, Miles. It's all wrong, but I do love you," I whispered, kissing him. I thrust my tongue in his mouth. I said the words, but it didn't matter to me that what we were doing was wrong and impossible. Nothing outside my room mattered to me. There was no age difference, no morality issue, and no regret. At that moment, I was right where I had dreamed of being for so long!

That was the beginning of our love affair. Like in the classroom, I was the teacher. I guided Miles to the pleasure zones of my body and showed him how to control his so that he could give and receive ultimate pleasure. We explored each other's bodies, learning every nook and cranny by heart. We wanted to know everything we could about each other, and we sought to do nothing but please.

Miles was a willing pupil, always anxious to learn. Sometimes, he surpassed my lessons, and he never held back his feelings for me. I found ultimate joy and satisfaction in the purity and innocence of his love. When we were alone together, I didn't think nor care about the fact that he was so young. To my way of thinking, age was only a number.

We talked, laughed, and loved with the abandon of irresponsible children; our love made even more special because it was forbidden. Miles treasured me, and I treasured him. There was nothing we wouldn't do for each other. Miles ran tedious and mundane errands for me without complaint. He wrote me beautiful, romantic emails, and even sent me gorgeous roses when he thought I needed cheering up about something. No mature lover had ever treated me as special as Miles treated me.

I couldn't help falling deeply in love with him. It was hard for me to keep from peeping my hold card when we were around other people, and he had confessed that it bothered him that he couldn't tell anyone how he felt about me. We both worried about the consequences should one of us slip up and reveal our illicit tryst. I was worried about everything: my job, the embarrassment, what would happen with Miles, and what would happen to me when I had to give him up.

Miles was more worried about me than about himself. He always told me that he would protect me and take care of me—as if I were a helpless little girl. His declarations only made me love him all the more, and I was acutely aware of how terrible it would be not to have him in my life—for any reason. It was insane—all of it. I told myself that many times.

I warned Miles that he should prepare himself for the day when we would have to end our relationship, because a love like ours simply wouldn't be allowed to last forever. Even though we were always extremely careful and very discreet, I knew we couldn't hide our affair too much longer. As it was, I was already getting twisted looks from the young girls who had crushes on Miles, and someone had even left an anonymous note on my desk calling me a "cradle robber."

Miles assured me that he hadn't told anyone about us, and that he wouldn't. But people weren't blind nor stupid, and they were beginning to whisper and speculate about the nature of our relationship. When I was not with Miles, I worried to no end about what would happen to us. I knew I should've been the strong one and do the sensible thing and end our affair before there was trouble. Still, I could never find the courage to put an end to it.

We went on for months, pretending to be normal lovers and treasuring our stolen moments together. One day I got a call from Miles' mother.

"You ought to be ashamed of yourself, Ms. Lindsay," she spat. I could feel her rolling her eyes at me through the phone. "I know that Miles is dating you, and I can't believe a woman your age—let alone a teacher who's supposed to be educating youth—would stoop so low. You should try sleeping with a man your own age. You're nothing but a lowdown Jezebel! I can't make Miles stop seeing you, but I can make a lot of trouble for you if you don't stop it!" She hung up before I could get a word in edgewise.

There was nothing I could say because what she said was right on point. I felt cheap and ashamed. I knew that everyone would feel like Mrs. Chandler did: that I was just a dirty older woman who was taking advantage of a much younger man, and that I was corrupting him morally. They wouldn't even try to understand how much I really loved Miles or why I loved him. Why wasn't I with someone who was my own age, they would wonder? What could a woman my age possibly find interesting about a much younger man—except sex, they'd assume. They'd turn something between two people deeply in love into something wanton and dirty.

I cried for hours after I hung up the phone with Mrs. Chandler. I vowed to break it off with Miles for both our sakes. I asked myself why I had let myself get involved in such a mess in the first place, but I knew the answer. Wrong or not, I loved Miles. I felt good with him—better than I had ever felt with another man, and I didn't want to give that up.

I told Miles about the call from his mother, and I even suggested to him that we end our relationship before things blew up around us.

"No! No one can tell us not to see each other. I'll explain what we have to my mother. It'll be all right. Don't worry, baby. I'm not going to stop seeing you, Sherry."

I didn't argue with Miles. I was glad he protested and refused to break it off. I loved him with everything inside me, but I was weak. I even questioned the quality of my own moral character after that. There had to be something innately wrong with me for me to be in love with so young a man. I berated myself. I should've been strong enough to walk away from something as wrong as what I was doing—something that was a virtual hotbed of trouble, but I couldn't.

Just as he promised me, Miles talked to his mother. I never asked him what she said, and he never volunteered. We simply continued our affair and ignored the obvious danger signs that were in our midst.

We spent every waking moment together, intensifying our relationship. We pretended that everything was fine and perfect—although we both knew that was far from the truth. I reminded him now and then that we couldn't expect things to go on the way they were forever. We both knew that someone or something would "out" us and put our affair on Front Street. We just didn't know how long we had or how it would happen.

I agonized over my responsibility as a thinking adult to allow things to get worse before making the break, but the moment never seemed to be right. So I kept putting off making that move.

One day, the decision of when or if to end the affair was abruptly taken out of my hands when I was called into the principal's office.

"Either you can accept an assignment in another school district—which by the way, we've already secured for you, Miss Lindsay—or you can resign from teaching and lose everything you've earned thus far," he explained, peering at me over the tops of his half moon glasses. Either way, we demand that you end this disgraceful relationship with Miles Chandler. His mother has already gone to the school board, and she's threatening to go to the media with the story about you and her son if it isn't stopped. If that happens, there could possibly even be some criminal charges levied against you. They might not hold up, and you might not go to jail, but your teaching career would be ruined. I'm sure you can imagine what such notoriety would do to you, this school, and to the boy. We don't need that. I'm sure you can see that. A scandal like this could ruin the rest of the young man's life."

I accepted the transfer. It meant leaving my job at the end of that week, and reporting to another district in a few weeks. I would get severance pay, and my pension would be transferred, but realistically, I was being run out of town! My love affair with my beloved Miles was over.

I didn't tell Miles about my meeting with the principal, nor that everything was over between us. For the next two days, it was hard for me to go on as if my life were unchanged. I was deeply depressed and heartbroken, but somehow, I managed to make it to the end of the week.

On Friday—my last day at the school—Miles came to my house for dinner as usual. I broiled two steaks, and we ate by candlelight in front of the fireplace. Miles was sad and quiet—barely eating anything, picking at his food. I was sure he knew something.

After we finished dinner, we relaxed on a blanket in front of the fire, and we held each other. We said nothing for a long time, then suddenly, he leaned over and kissed me passionately. I smiled up at him, but he wasn't smiling. He stroked my hair and sighed.

"Who's going to take care of you?" He whispered.

I laid my hand on top of his and sighed, loving him more than ever fore thinking about my future.

"I love you, Miles," I said, wrapping my arms around him. "I'll be fine," I added.

His arms tightened around me, and I felt his heart pound furiously through his shirt.

"Don't leave, Sherry. Please don't leave." His voice trembled. "I love you. I'll make all of them leave us alone. It's our business what we do with each other. Don't let them make you leave."

I hugged him to my bosom and sighed.

"I have to go, Miles."

"Then, I'm going with you."

"No, Miles. You can't. It would only make things worse. It's over, Miles. We both knew this day would come. Let's enjoy what we had and never forget it. Let's not make it any harder than it already is. We don't have any choice in the matter."

"You're giving up too easily. Nobody can tell us to stop loving each other. I'll don't want to go on without you, Sherry!" He rocked me back and forth. Tears welled up in his eyes. "I'll die without you," he repeated, his voice breaking.

My own eyes filled up, and I shook my head in the negative—refusing to give into him again. "Don't say that, Miles. And don't think it, either. I have to leave here, sweetheart. I don't want to, but I have to. You could be the subject of a lot of humiliation, and I could go to jail if I don't leave."

We were both crying now, and I wrapped my arms around him, holding him tightly. His body shook violently, his hurt radiating to me like fire.

"Please understand and don't say you can't live without me. I've already caused you enough harm. If you do something to yourself because of me, I'll never forgive myself. I've never been happier in my life, Miles. You've given me the finest love I've ever known. I've honestly never loved anyone the way I love you. No one can ever take that away from us. But, right now, there's nothing else we can do except what they want us to do."

I felt his body trembling, then he raised up and shook me a little.

"I'm going with you. I don't care where it is. I can do what I want and with whomever I want. I can't stand the thought of not seeing you, not being with you, Sherry!"

"No, Miles," I whispered, shaking my head. "If you go with me, we'll still have the same problems. Things might be okay in a few months, but there are a lot of terrible things that could happen in the meantime. Maybe one day, we'll get another chance. Maybe later . . . if we haven't met anyone else."

"I don't want anyone else! I don't want you to be with anyone else! I don't want to lose you! We can do something! You're giving up without a fight!" Miles yelled, anger dripping from his voice. He stood up and turned his back to me, kicking at the wood chips that had fallen from the fireplace.

I saw his shoulders rise and fall, and I knew he was still upset. I left him alone for a few minutes, venting my own pain and anguish through my tears. Then, I stood up and put my arms around him—urging him to look at me. I wiped at the tears on his face, then at my own.

"I love you, Miles Chandler," I whispered and pulled him down to the blanket. "Make love to me," I whispered again as we embraced.

Miles pulled me close, and he began undressing me, wiping at his tears every now and then. He undressed and lay beside me, caressing me all over—as if he were trying to memorize every inch of my body. I did the same to him, feeling his manhood harden almost immediately. We made love with an urgency that seemed almost surreal. We made love several times that evening, cuddling tightly. Then we fell asleep in each other's arms. Both of us were emotionally spent. I awakened shortly before midnight, and I sent Miles home. I never saw him again.

That was four years ago. I moved to the town where my teaching job was waiting, but I couldn't bring myself to take it. Instead, I went to real estate school, l and secured my license, and I became a broker. I found out that I really enjoyed and making deals and that I had a real knack for finding just the right property for the right people. I met my husband when I was closing a real estate deal with another company where he was an agent.

We have a great marriage. He's caring, attentive, loving, and dependable, but hardly a day goes by that I don't think about my love affair with Miles Chandler and compare what we had with what I have with my husband now. Somehow, I know that I'll never have anything as sweet and tender as the love I had with Miles. I'd like to think that wherever he is, I still remain an important part of his past, too. I've never once regretted my affair with him, although I've never told anyone about it. It's not that I'm ashamed of it. It's just that I know that no one would understand my being in love with a young man almost ten years younger than me, and I prefer not to have to try and explain.

I know that Miles loved me very much and that I loved him just as much. As long as I live, I'll be able to look back on that time in my life and treasure it with all my heart. I still have the wonderful emails and the hordes of beautiful memories to warm me when I feel down or caught up in the complexities of life. There is an indelible picture of Miles etched in my heart.

Maybe Miles and I will meet again someday. I don't even imagine that we could take up where we left off—even if I weren't a married woman now, but in a secret room of my heart—just as I promised Miles, I will always love him and nothing and no one can ever take that away from me!

THE END

JEALOUS AND DERANGED
She Tried To Kill Me… Over Her Man!

I spun around, stunned, as I felt a fist connect with the back of my head. My first thought was that I was being mugged. It was eleven p.m., and I was a block away from my apartment building. I had just come back from my cousin's house a couple of blocks away, and had thought that the walk home would be uneventful. I'd lived in this Fort Greene neighborhood for a year, and had never had a problem before. Until that night.

Yet, I was about to find out that I had enemies I wasn't even aware of. When I turned around and looked into the eyes of my attacker, I saw that it was the girl who had been standing in front of my building that afternoon.

"You wanna mess with someone else's man, bitch? He don't want you; you best step!"

The brown-skinned girl pulled her fist back, preparing to hit me again. But that time, I was ready for her. I grabbed her hand, and held on. I used my other hand to snag a fistful of her braids.

"I don't know what you're talking about," I said, holding on tight. "But you'd better keep your hands to yourself!" I tightened my grip as the girl struggled, cursing at me to let her hair go. "I'm not letting you go until you tell me what your problem is." I pulled her closer to me. "You lucky I don't mess your butt up out here!"

At that moment, I looked up to see a bunch of girls standing a few feet away. I didn't know whether they were friends of hers or not, but I knew if I held on tightly enough, they wouldn't dare step over to me. Girls like that—cowards all of them—ran in packs.

Finally, the girl stopped moving. "Let me go so we can talk," she whispered.

Carefully, I disentangled my hands from her head, and took a step back. "You hit me again, and you're going down," I said.

The girl sucked her teeth and put her hands on her hips. "Don't mess around and get yourself jumped. You need to leave other women's men alone." She motioned to the girls I noticed earlier. "They got my back. One word, and you're going to get beat down out here!"

I had thought that I'd left childhood stuff like that behind me, years ago. I was twenty-four, and hadn't been in a fight in nearly ten years. It was obvious, though, that this girl was a bit younger than me, and still raring to go.

"Who's your man?" I asked. "I don't even have a boyfriend, honey.

43

You must have me mistaken for somebody else."

But she shook her head.

"Rashan Powell. Every time I come around here, you're talking to him. You up in his face. I asked around—my cousin lives in your building—and she said you always be hanging around him." She stuck her finger in my face. "You need to leave him alone. Seriously, Miss Connie. And I'm only telling you this once."

My first reaction was to throw down my bag and beat her where she stood. I wasn't afraid of her or her friends. But this girl not only knew where I lived; she also knew my name. I decided to play it cool.

"Yeah, I know Rashan. The guy with the bald head, right? We talk. But that's it. I'm not trying to get with him."

She rolled her eyes.

"My man is fine. You expect me to believe that you not trying to get with him?"

"Yep," I said. "I don't like Rashan like that." I turned to walk away, but decided to leave her with something to remember. "But every time he and I talk, he comes up to me."

After she'd attacked me, and I put her in her place, I assumed that the drama was over. But the girl—I found out that her name was Nicole—began calling my house into the wee hours of the morning, and hanging outside in front of my building—even though she didn't live there.

One day, I walked past her and her friends and she called out to me. "Seen Rashan today, Connie? I did." She cackled. "He's gonna come back and be with me." A group of guys blared music and watched us, puffing marijuana and laughing their heads off in their broken down Honda Accord. "Ah, they still got beef!" one yelled out, pointing at me.

I kept walking, but turned long enough to say, "I'm happy if you're happy. Don't nobody want your man!"

She poked her fingers on the loops of her tight jean shorts before running her hands over her saggy bosom. "You want him, bitch. But he wants me—he wants this!" She slapped her own backside, and her friends collapsed into fits of laughter.

Within a week of the unprovoked attack, I ran into Rashan—a man I barely knew, but whose very existence would bring me trouble for months to come.

"Hey, Connie. How you doing?"

I shrugged, and looked around. Nicole was nowhere in sight that day, but I knew that she had been in the building.

"Your girlfriend tried to fight me the other day."

"Wait, Connie. I don't even have a girlfriend!"

He leaned against the door of our building, and only looked away

44

to nod at a group of boys crossing the street.

"Does the name 'Nicole' ring any bells?"

When his mouth went slack and he nodded, I pressed on.

"She hit me in the back of the head and tried to have her preteen posse jump me! The girl is crazy, Rashan, but I handled it. You best tell that girl to stay out of my way. If she bothers me again, I'm prepared to make things serious."

Rashan smiled at me. "Look, I'm sorry about that. Nicole and I broke up nearly four months ago, but she won't leave me alone. She thinks every woman I speak to is my new girlfriend." He apologized again and asked me if I gotten hurt. "I told her to stay away from me, but she has friends who live in the building. I'll talk to her, again."

"Sounds good, Rashan," I grinned. "And I suggest you give your next girlfriend a background check."

After that conversation, I didn't see Nicole for a couple of weeks. I figured that Rashan had talked her into leaving me alone. Still, I wasn't that thrilled when he stopped me outside to talk. One day, I told him that I thought it was best if we weren't seen together in public. "I'm in no mood for foolishness," I told him. "I'm grown, and I don't feel the need to have to prove myself like I'm on a playground or something."

He smiled at me, and I couldn't help but melt into his pretty brown eyes. His skin was a rich dark chocolate, and idly, I wondered what he might taste like.

"She hasn't been hanging around much, anymore," he said. "I explained—for the thirty-sixth time—that what we had is over. I also told her that you and I are just friends."

"What a relief," I said, a sarcastic edge to my voice. "So what does that mean? I don't have to worry about her trying to hit me in the head, anymore?"

"Actually, she said the next time she'd come at you with a razor."

"Are you serious?" I looked around before taking a step back. The usual suspects stood in front of my building. But there was no sign of Nicole and her friends. "She's talking about trying to slice me up, Rashan?"

He put his hands up in a placating gesture.

"Don't worry. She only said that before I calmed her down."

"And how were you able to do that?"

"I told her you weren't my type—that you were ugly."

I must have looked horrified, because he stepped closer in and whispered into my ear. "Girl, don't worry; you know you're fine. But Nicole is just so crazy. The only way I got her to believe I wasn't interested in you, was to tell her you weren't hot."

For some reason, I felt relieved. Secretly, I cared very much what

45

this hood thought about my looks. He was very good looking in a rugged sort of way. I was glad he found me attractive. Why am I thinking this way? I asked myself. It doesn't matter what he thinks, as long as that little hood rat stayed away from me! "Thanks, Rashan," I said, feeling silly. "Hopefully, she'll listen to you this time. I don't need anymore drama."

But three days later, as soon as I had started to feel safe again, I opened my apartment door only to see Nicole standing there! I was immediately on guard. Putting on my toughest face, I asked, "What the hell do you want?"

"Rashan," she answered, her caramel skin burning bright crimson. "And I want you to leave him alone!"

"How many times do I have to tell you that I don't want him?"

She stuck a finger in my face. "Yeah, you said that the last time I stepped to your dumb behind. Yet and still, every time I'm not around, I get word that you outside trying to kick it with him, again!" A vein above her eye jumped, and I realized then that this teenager was indeed crazy.

"Look, I'm not going to tell you again, little girl," I huffed, tired of her games. "Get from in front of my door. I don't have to explain myself to you. And what's more—I can talk to anybody I damn well please!"

Her eyes narrowed at me, and she puffed up her chest. "You saying you gon' keep messing with him? That I'm gonna have to mess you up out here? Because I will, you know. You ain't nobody around here; don't nobody know you or care what happens to you!"

I rolled my eyes.

"Then you shouldn't care, either! I don't even know you. Why are you constantly in my face?"

"If you would leave my man—"

"He's not your man, Nicole! He told me that. He's told you that, and it's pitiful that you're chasing him around, and starting fights with people. There are other men out here, girl." I lowered my voice and strived to build a sort of understanding with her. "You are a pretty girl; you should find somebody who wants to be with you."

"Rashan does want to be with me, slut! If you would just stay the hell out of our lives!" Suddenly, her hand shot up, and the sight of metal caught my eye.

I stepped back, gamely missing her first slash; but the second connected with my arm. I cried out, and closed the door just as she rampaged forward, intent on slitting me open. "I'm calling the police!" I screamed through the door. "I mean it, Nicole!"

"Bitch, I'll be long gone before they come. And nobody around here is gonna help you, so you best save your dime!" Through my keyhole I watched her hitch up her too-large pants and strut down the hallway. She had a wide smile on her face. *The little bitch thinks she's won!* I thought.

I really wanted to take off after her and show her what a good fight looked like. But I held my ground because of the blood streaming down my arm. I felt light-headed, and stumbled back to sit on my sofa. Looking down at my slashed T-shirt sleeve, I saw a pool of bright red blood congealing, there. My hands shaking, I picked up my phone to call an ambulance.

When I got to the emergency room, the police were waiting for me. So was Rashan. I was hustled into a small room where an ER nurse with a sour expression stitched me up. I tried to ask her questions about scarring and doctor's appointments. "You'll be fine, Miss Renault," she said, looking at my wristband. "You have fourteen stitches, all of which will come out in a couple of weeks." She passed me an appointment sheet and a two-day prescription for a painkiller. She frowned before pushing me toward the door. "The police are waiting for you."

When I got to the waiting room, two detectives stood and approached me. Rashan hovered in the background, trying not to get into anyone's way. Despite the air conditioning, he was sweating terribly, and his black T-shirt clung to his muscular body.

"Can you identify you assailant in a line-up?" the taller detective asked.

"Was the incident personal?"

"How do you know her?"

They threw so many questions at me, that my head began to spin. I sat down and answered each as best I could, and tried to mention Rashan's involvement as little as possible. After a few minutes though, he stepped forward to help me out.

"Nicole Sampson is my ex-girlfriend. She's the one who did this to Connie. I can tell you where she lives, and where to find her if she's not home."

The detectives looked him up and down.

"Would you like to come down to the station with us? You know, to talk about this situation?"

Rashan shook his head.

"No. I'll call or come down in the morning." He pointed at me. "I'm here to support this lady. You ready for a ride home, Connie?"

I looked between him and the two cops. My arm was sore, and I was tired of answering questions. "Thanks, I could use a ride," I said.

Rashan helped me buckle my seatbelt. "You all right?"

"Yep. I just want to get outta here." I turned to look out the window—a signal that I didn't want to talk. But my disinterest didn't stop him.

"I'm so sorry about this mess, Connie. That's why I went down to talk to the cops. Nicole's going to have to do some time, for sure."

I shook my head. "Isn't she underage? Yeah, she'll do some time, but not much."

"Couldn't we have her tried as an adult?"

I laughed.

"You've been watching too many crime shows, Rashan. She's not going to be tried as anything. Her public defender will probably plead her down to some kiddie charge, and she'll do a year in juvenile detention, and be forced to see a therapist for anger management."

After that, we rode back to the apartment building in silence. It was only after he'd parked the car when he asked a question. "Why don't you come up to my apartment, Connie?"

Despite knowing that cops were on her scent, I looked around, fully expecting Nicole to slink out of the shadows, wielding a knife.

"I don't think that's a good idea, Rashan."

"Why not? You've had a hard night, and that's mostly my fault." He stepped forward and pulled me close to him. "Come in for a while. Let me take care of you."

Swallowing the lump forming in my throat, I stepped into the elevator, and rode past my apartment on the fourth floor. When we stopped on the seventh, we stepped out.

I don't know what I expected Rashan's apartment to be like, but I was completely surprised by what I saw. His living room was painted in a deep, warm shade of red, and it was spotless. He walked me over to the sofa and sat me down.

"How's your arm doing?"

"It doesn't hurt that bad," I admitted. "I mean, there's obviously discomfort—I got stabbed—but it's more of a burning itch than a terrible pain."

"Good," he said. "Give me a minute. I'm gonna go get us something to eat."

"Okay, Rashan."

I looked at my watch. It was just after ten. I couldn't believe that only four hours had passed since Nicole had attacked me. A few minutes later, my young host came out of his kitchen carrying two plates. "I hope you like turkey and cheese," he said, as he sat a sandwich in front of me.

"Sure do." I bit down and was delighted by the taste. He'd added lettuce, tomato, and jalapeno peppers as well as mayonnaise and a dab of mustard. The cheese was provolone, which was one of my favorites. "If I had known you could cook, I would have visited months ago!" I joked.

"Oh yeah?" he said, wiping a napkin across his full mouth. "Well, if I had known that I could have lured you up here with sandwich meats, I would have done it a long time ago!"

When we finished eating, I tried to stand and take my plate into the kitchen, but Rashan stopped me. "I'll get that in a minute," he said. "Let's talk a while."

The tone of his voice alerted me to the seriousness of the topic.

"What about?"

"The reason we're here. The reason Nicole went nuts on you."

I took a deep breath. "She didn't go nuts; that's chile is nuts! If I didn't step back when I did, I'd probably be dead, or at least seriously cut up."

"I'm sorry," he said.

"You sound like a broken record, I snapped. "It's not your fault—not really. You just need better taste in women."

He leaned in real close.

"I think my taste is improving," he whispered. "That's why Nicole is so jealous. . . ."

"But there's nothing between us," I said, searching his face. "I've told her that over and over. Hell, before she stepped to me that first time, I didn't even know your name!"

"But you know it, now," his hand descended upon my knee. "And you know I like you."

"Rashan . . . I don't think this is a good idea," I choked out. But it was too late; his hands were all over me, and I can't say I didn't like it. Together, we sank back into the sofa, and I whimpered as he kissed me until my lips felt swollen. His hands were rough as they pulled up my jean skirt, and I didn't hesitate to help him remove his belt and peel out of his pants.

"Watch your arm," he said, positioning my body so that I wasn't lying directly on my wound. "You don't want it to get infected." He bent to kiss me again, and for a moment, I was lost in the heat of his body.

Slowly, I reached up and ran a hand over the tiny braids that dotted his scalp, and was surprised at his response. He inhaled deeply, and his eyes dilated. "I love to have my head rubbed. The feel of a woman's hand in my hair makes me crazy." He bent forward so that I could massage him more, and my heart raced at the feel of his body tensing over mine.

Soon, my hands were unrolling a condom and pushing it over the head of his straining erection. I stroked the sheath along his hardness, rolling in an upward motion. Rashan leaned up to allow my hands to work, sucking in his breath as my fingers brushed his taut member. He bent down and reclaimed my lips, pulling my legs across his broad shoulders.

"You ready?" he whispered upon my lips, his eyes searching mine.

"Yes, Rashan. I'm ready."

That's when he burrowed inside me, merging our flesh until it became one. I gasped, and tightened around him, rocking against him in a rhythmic ride. Over and over, his hardness opened me, and I pumped to meet him. I was breathless, helpless—a shaking quivering mess as I shuddered through his loving assault. My eyes fluttered to look at him as his hips ground into me, but each of his thrusts sent me into such a pleasurable place that I was forced to close them, succumbing to the heat of his desire.

My insides collapsed and soared as waves of pleasure tore through me. I bucked against him, crying out my devastation, mewling like a wounded animal. With a low growl, Rashan bit out his orgasm, pulling me close to him.

We lay together for a while, our breathing slowing, and our skin cooling off. As the enormity of what I'd done sunk into my consciousness, I patted him on his chest. "Get up, now; please."

"What's the problem, Connie?" He was still inside me, and it seemed there was no other place he'd rather be. "I was just resting up for round two."

"There won't be any round two!" I bit out, roughly shoving at him. "Get up, now!"

"Why are you acting like this?"

His eyes were questioning.

I stood and pulled my skirt over my thighs. I could still feel him inside of me, a phantom thickness sliding through my depths.

"You're trouble, Rashan, and that's the last thing I need. The first few times I ran into your ex, at least I'd been telling the truth when I told her I wasn't messing around with you." My eyes were wild. "But now that we've slept together, things can only get more complicated."

He stood to block my path, and I couldn't help but look at the fine thickness of his lips and remember how they had felt on my body.

"I can handle Nicole."

"You think so? She's obsessed, Rashan. She's not trying to beat you up—maybe even kill you; she saves her wrath for me." I sidestepped him. "For all I know, it's all over the complex that I've been up in your apartment. When she finds out, she's gonna want blood!"

He grabbed my wrists and pulled me to him. His eyes were sad, but some of the lusty feelings from earlier still hung around.

"I know you ain't afraid of Nicole and her gang of thugs. They're just kids; there's no reason for you to be scared."

I pulled free.

"That's right; they're just kids, Rashan. That's what worries me the most about you. What were you doing messing with her in the first place? You're twenty-two years old; she's sixteen. You should have known better!"

His eyes narrowed. "If I wanted to be lectured about the women I dated, I'd go see my mother," he said, his voice hard. "Yeah, Nicole was a mistake—one I look back on now and wish I hadn't made." He looked down at the floor, and his fists clenched at his sides. "But I've been honest with her, Connie. And now, I'm being honest with you. I want to see you—build something. I just want a chance."

I stalked to the door. "I don't see how we can make things worse. If I see you, I'll be constantly harassed—maybe even attacked, again. I'm not willing to chance that, Rashan." I stepped into the hall and closed the door behind me.

That night, my phone rang off the hook. I let my answering machine pick up the messages, and I wasn't surprised to hear over a dozen messages from Nicole and her crew the next day.

When I spoke to the police, they admitted there wasn't much they could do. "We haven't been able to track her down, Miss Renault. Nicole Bryant has relatives all throughout the tri-state area, and some in Virginia and North Carolina. She could be anywhere, by now." The cop who'd done most of the talking at the hospital ran a hand through his thinning hair. "Was there a number left on your caller ID?"

"All the calls came in as blocked or as a private number."

He shook his head.

"We have men going out to her usual haunts, and we're interviewing her family and friends." He shrugged. "It's the best we can do, right now. When we find her, you'll be the first to know."

"So what am I supposed to do?" I turned in my seat and pushed up my T-shirt. I made sure he saw the ugly black stitches crisscrossing my bruised flesh. "Look at what she did to me! Am I supposed to wait for her to come back and finish the job?"

"I doubt she'll come back to try and harm you again, Miss Renault. She's on the run—hiding with someone. Try to go back to living normally. Before you know it, time will pass and after we've caught up with her, this situation won't seem so upsetting."

I stood and left the station as quickly as I could. The detective had no regard for me or what I was feeling; he definitely didn't give a damn about my safety. He might as well have said, "Those are the dangers of living in the projects, Miss Renault," for all the interest he showed me.

I took a couple of days off work and spent them hiding out in my apartment. Suddenly, I'd become the criminal. I also had to curse out Rashan a few times after he'd turned up at my door.

"I need to talk to you," he said one day around midnight, but I stubbornly kept the door bolted.

"Get away from my door!" I hissed. "Leave me alone!"

Two weeks later, my cousin told me there was a vacancy on the second floor of a private house next door to her. I interviewed for the apartment, passed the background check, and very quietly left Rashan and his crazy ex-girlfriend in the past!

THE END

JAILBAIT!
He Didn't Know I Was Fifteen
Until The Next Morning!

Since it was Saturday night, all my friends were going out to a nightclub. I really didn't want to go because we all were under eighteen, and it was embarrassing at times when we got asked for identification. However, I had let Joyce talk me into it, so I couldn't back out. Furthermore, Joyce and her sister, Laurel, were paying for the drinks, provided we got in. The three of us were supposed to meet two more of our friends, Jackie and Darla, at the club.

I wore a new outfit, high heels, and extra makeup to help me look older.

When we arrived at the club there was a crowd standing outside the back door. Jackie had filled us in on what little details she knew about a fight that was about to take place. We had managed to squeeze through the crowd to see if the dispute involved anyone we knew. They were strangers: a cute guy dressed in a suit and tie was about to fight a man twice his size. The situation was rather humorous because the smaller guy was talking loud and dancing around while punching at the air, as if he knew for sure that he was going to win. There were four other men, also dressed in suits, standing to the side of him as if they were going to assist him if something went wrong. I couldn't understand it, the five of them looked like businessmen who should have been sitting behind a desk instead of being at a nightclub about to fight.

The larger man looked more like a professional wrestler on television. When he took off his coat and revealed all of his muscles, I mumbled a prayer to myself for the smaller man. When he took off his coat, he revealed a nice little neat vest holding together skin and bones.

Everyone stepped further into the alley and formed a circle around the two. Jackie didn't know exactly what they were going to fight about, but whatever the reason, they were serious.

The smaller man began dancing around again as if he were a champion boxer. I figured, perhaps he knew karate or something and just might have a chance.

The big man put his fists up and started for the smaller man. Then, the smaller man's friends stepped forward. I closed my eyes. "Thank God, they are not going to let him fight," I whispered. However, to my surprise, they only wanted to inform the big man that if he lost, they were taking his belongings, starting with his watch. That made me wonder what type of dudes they really were.

I whispered to Jackie, "This doesn't make any sense. Why doesn't one of his friends fight the big guy for him since all four of them are about his size?"

"Someone should stop it," Jackie answered.

Just then, one of the four moved over and started a conversation with Laurel. I was about to go closer and see what was up, when the smaller man started bobbing and waving.

The big man got closer to him, and asked, "Are you ready, clown?"

"Are you ready?" the smaller man responded.

"Yeah!"

"Well, let's go then! " the smaller man said with a nod.

The big man drew back and threw a punch that would have surely stopped a champion heavyweight boxer. The small guy stood there frozen, he didn't move or duck and caught it flush on the chin.

The next thing I knew, everything was happening so fast. The smaller man's friends were picking him up unconscious off the ground. Sometime in between the fight, Laurel had arranged with the guy she was talking to for us to ride with them.

The five of them were riding in two black cars with out-of-state license plates. Linda and I got in one of the cars. The small guy was still unconscious, so we laid him in the back with his head in my lap and his feet in Linda's lap. Our three other friends and two of them role in the other car in front of us.

I couldn't believe it; we were on our way to their hotel room. I wasn't a virgin, but I had never gone to a hotel before in my life.

The small guy began to gain consciousness.

"He's waking up," I said. He looked up at me and I gave a half smile and asked, "How do you feel?"

"My eye is killing me," he said. "Is it real big?"

"Yes," I replied.

His friend on the passenger side turned around, and looked at him. "I hope you're satisfied. You got beat up. Now, maybe you'll be cool," he told him.

"What makes it so bad, you had to go in there and pick out the biggest dude in the place to mess with," the driver added without turning around.

I could sense from their tone of voices that they were good friends and were just teasing him. "By the way you were talking, I thought you knew karate," I couldn't help saying.

He looked up at me. "Who asked you?" he said. "And by the way, who are you?" He tried to sit up but fell back into my lap.

My friend laughed lightly at his remark. He looked at her, as if at

54

first he didn't know that she was there. "Who are you?" he asked her.

Before she could answer, the one on the passenger side picked up a CB receiver. "Hey, I wanted to let you know that the World Champion is now conscious," he said into the receiver. "Ali Junior. Over."

A voice came over the CB and I had a hunch it was coming from the other car.

"Ask Tony, Ali, what happened to his plan. Over."

Tony was the little guy. He sat up between my friend and me and asked his friend for the receiver, then he spoke into it. "Say, Clayton, I did have a plan, but I don't know what happened. Over." Everyone began to laugh.

Robert was the name of the man on the passenger side. He took the receiver back. "Yeah, he had a plan, but when that dude hit him, he forgot about it and everything else."

Everyone began laughing again while Tony put his head back in my lap.

"Robert, what happened back there?" Tony asked.

"The man hit you with a right that shook the earth," Robert answered.

"Oh, yeah? I didn't remember anything after I saw his fist coming towards my face," Tony said. "Then was that it?"

I looked down into his face. He looked so sweet with his head lying comfortably on my lap. "No, you got back up mumbling and trying to talk more mess," I said with a smile.

Robert turned back to face him. "Then he drew back and knocked fire from you again." Robert laughed and turned back to face the road.

"I said to myself, 'Oh, please, don't let this nut get up again'," I said.

"Did I stay down?" Tony asked innocently.

I laughed. "No. Your crazy self got right back up, and this time swinging in front of you while the dude was standing in back of you."

"Did I finally turn around and hit him?"

"No," the driver replied. "But you did turn around, and he drew back and hit you again and lifted you about three feet up into the air."

"Don't tell me I got up again?" he asked.

"Yeah, you got up, but not by yourself. You were out cold, so your friends picked you up and carried you to the car," I told him.

"Where did you come from?" he asked me.

Before I could answer, the driver spoke up. "They wanted to ride, and there are three more in the other car."

"I must have looked pretty good when that dude was knocking me around," he said and laughed.

I was enjoying myself and I liked his sense of humor.

Robert chuckled. "Yeah, you were. Especially the last time he hit you. You looked so pretty flying through the air that I fell in love with you."

Tony closed his eyes. "Are all of the women for me?" he asked.

"No. You didn't look that good," Robert replied. "Only the one holding your head, and that's because she left her glasses at home."

Tony opened his eyes, looked up at me, and smiled. "Well, all is well that ends well. At least I got a pretty belly warmer to make me feel better when I get so my hotel room."

I had to laugh because I had never heard the term 'belly warmer.'

When we arrived at the hotel, Robert and Mark had to help Tony in. As we walked through the lobby, people stopped and stared.

I was walking in back of Tony, carrying his coat when an older, light-skinned woman walked past him. "Did you win?" she asked.

"Well, you know me," Tony said.

She looked to be about twenty-two years old, pretty, and had long black hair. The way she was dressed was evidence that she worked there. I could also tell by the look in her eyes that she liked him. Nevertheless, so did I. I liked everything about him and I was going to hold on and make him mine, even with stiff competition.

When we got upstairs, they each had their own room. We went to Tony's room first. Everything was going smoothly; they hadn't questioned our ages and were treating us with the utmost respect.

Tony had put ice on his eye to reduce the swelling. After talking and drinking ice cold, imported champagne, each of my friends paired off with one of them and eventually left and went to their room, leaving Tony and me alone. I felt I had the pick of the bunch.

Tony told me that he was going to take a bath, and invited me to join him.

I was nervous at first and had second thoughts. However, I figured that was what an older woman would do, because he asked with confidence that I would say yes.

I agreed and he led me to the bathroom by the hand. It was a large bathroom with a sunken tub in the middle of the floor, big enough to accommodate five people. Everything was blue, my favorite color, with mirrors on the ceiling and the walls around the tub area.

He took off his shirt and allowed it to drop to the floor. Then he pulled me to him, and began kissing me gently while undressing me. When he got my top off, he began caressing me while carefully lowering my skirt. Any other time, I wouldn't have went that far with a man that I had just met. Actually, he wasn't stripping me fast enough.

Moaning softly, I began helping him off with his pants; that was all I could do to keep from screaming out for his touch.

The water was lukewarm, and the bubbles were plentiful. He took me in his arms and began kissing my neck and caressing my body.

Colors flashed, and shivers shot up and down my spine. Suddenly, there was a knock at the door.

He brought his mouth from mine. "Look, I'll be right back. Don't you dare move," he whispered, and then kissed me again. He stood up, wrapped a towel around him, and walked out. He had left the bathroom door open and when he opened the other door, I heard a lady's voice.

"Hello," she said. "I came by to make you feel better." Then she walked past the bathroom and stopped at the bathroom door when she saw me. It was the same lady that was in the lobby. I knew I was right. She either wanted him or already had a thing with him. Whatever the case was, tonight she was too late. Although I was much younger than her, I now had my hooks in him and wasn't loosening my grip. I had learned about men from my mother. She kept a hold on my daddy until the day he died. Mama drilled in me, and my sister, to go out and get what we wanted. Once we got it, she had shown us how to keep it.

"Oh, I see you already have something to keep your company!" she emphasized.

I turned to face her. I found no need for me to get upset; after all, I had what I wanted. For that matter, what she wanted. So I leaned back, and said, "Hello," and offered a pleasant smile.

She didn't say anything She just slung her head one way, a hip the other way, and walked back towards him as he now stood in my view.

"I'll be back tomorrow," she said to him, and stood on her toes and kissed him.

Now I knew that whatever type of relationship they had, he didn't have any commitments to her.

He started with that cute sense of humor. "You don't have to go now, there's room in the tub for the three of us, and then more."

At least, I hoped he was being humorous, because there was no way I was going to share anything with her.

"That's all right." She smiled and shook her head. "Now I see why you got your eye blackened, probably for saying something you wasn't supposed to."

"Could be," he said. "But I know one thing, it wasn't for having two women in the tub with me."

From his gentle touch and the thrilling mood that it had me in, plus the champagne I wanted to laugh about how smoothly he was handling the situation.

"That's because I wasn't one of them," she said. Then she swung her head as if to show off her hair, and started toward the entrance door. He went behind her to open the door

Then I heard her say, "I'll be by tomorrow. Make sure all the filth is out of your tub, and out of your room. Okay?"

"Good-bye," he said, laughed lightly, and closed the door.

I didn't care about her smart remarks. She still left. Besides, while I would enjoy myself for the rest of the night, she would no doubt have me on her mind.

When he got back in the tub, he leaned back and looked in my eyes. "Why do they call you Sugar?" he asked.

"I don't know. Why? You don't like it?" I took his hand into mine.

"It doesn't matter what I like. You're the one who has to answer to it."

"Oh, you don't like it?" I pulled my hand back from his, and splashed a little water on him.

Then to my surprise he said, "It sounds like a name for a horse." He laughed. "You know. Whoa, Sugar, whoa!"

"No, I don't know." I giggled, stood up, and watched his eyes search the full length of my body.

"You have a beautiful, well-developed body," he said.

"Thank you." I blushed as I stepped out of the tub, and began drying off.

He then asked the question that was well overdue. "How old are you?"

Keeping my back to him, I answered over my shoulder, 'Twenty'."

"You don't look twenty," he said, and stood up. "I mean, your body looks twenty, but your face, well, it looks seventeen." Without drying off, he walked into the other room.

I came out with a towel around me to find him lying on top of the blanket, sipping on another drink. "Look at you," I said. "You're soaking wet." I took off my towel, and slowly and teasingly, I crawled onto the bed and began drying him off. Watching him get excited from my touch made body flare into full flame.

He took me in his arms, began kissing me, and rolled me over on my back. He began kissing my body as no man had ever kissed me before. It made me go wild; my whole body began to tremble, and colored lights began to explode in my head.

No matter what happened now, the mood was so intense that there was no coercion in the wonderful process he had started.

Since he thought that much of me, I figured he was just as good and deserved the same royal treatment. He lay on his back, and I began to work my way down his body. I couldn't depend strictly on my tongue to find the threshold of his sensitivity, so I used my hands to guide me. We made love until we just laid there holding each other. I never felt so totally satisfied. I kissed him on his chest and we basked in the afterglow of love.

I finally dozed off, and the last thing I remembered was him lying on his back, in deep thought.

I didn't know how long I was asleep before he awakened me. "Why did you lie to me about your age?" he asked, as if addressing a girl instead of a mature woman.

"What's wrong with you?" I was puzzled until I looked in his hand.

"Whatís wrong with me? What's wrong with you, is the question!" he yelled. "Are you trying to get me put under the jail house? You're just a baby."

I didn't have the slightest idea of what he had been looking for, but he had searched through my purse and found my student identification card showing my true age. I sat up, not knowing what to say, but really wanting to question him about going into my purse. I finally uttered, "Look, I didn't notice your complaining before."

"I didn't know you were fifteen, either."

"Well, does it matter?" l was hoping he would look at my maturity and forget about my age.

"Yeah, it matters!"

I moved closer to him because I wanted it to go further than just a one-night thing. "Let me put it to you like this: after what we just did, isn't it a little late to complain?"

"No, it's not too late." Then he looked at my ID card again and added, "You should be in school!"

I was still feeling great from the ride of thrills that he had taken me on. Since he was angry and blowing off steam, I figured I couldn't talk to him now. However, perhaps, I could reason with him in the morning.

"I learned more tonight from you than I could ever learn in any old school!" I said teasingly. I laid back down and turned my back to him.

He became more upset. "Look, don't say you learned anything from me. In fact, don't even say you know me!"

I tried to keep from laughing, because he was still sounding cute.

"Good night, and believe me, it was a good night," I said.

"Oh. You think this is funny? If it wasn't so late, I would take you home right now."

"Quit crying. You know you want me to stay until morning. If I got up to leave right now, you'd fall out."

"Well, get up and try me!"

"Donít push your luck." I laughed. "Or I will."

"You've got a sassy mouth to be so young."

"Oh, now you're complaining about my mouth."

He was now calming down or becoming tired or running out of words.

Nevertheless, I still enjoyed being in his presence, no matter what mood he was in.

"Look, go back to sleep," he said.

"Don't get upset, Pops, everything is all right. I wouldn't have come if I thought it would get either of us in trouble. So good night."

"Yeah, good night." He got under the blanket and turned his back to me. He lay there for about five minutes before it registered that I'd called him 'Pops.'"

"I'm not 'Pops,' either!" he exclaimed.

With my back still to him, I couldn't keep from laughing. "You're kind of late, aren't you?"

He took a deep breath, but didn't say anything.

I rolled over and touched his back. "That's all right, though. You'll make it. Besides, I have something for you in the morning."

"A good-bye, I hope."

"It will be good, and it will get you by, but it won't be good-bye."

When morning arrived, I was awakened by a knock at the door. He was already up, dressed, and was on his way to open it. It was Joyce, the rest of the girls, and his friends. None of the other girls had been questioned about their ages. However, he wasted very little time telling his friends my age. Then they became suspicious and asked to see everyone's identification cards. It was revealed that, at sixteen, Joyce was the oldest of us all. They became angry, and Tony ordered them to take us home.

I took the towel, wrapped myself, and went in the bathroom and got dressed.

Everyone was riding except Tony. I supposed he didn't want to be seen with us. They all left and said they would wait for me in the car.

Tony and I were alone with the door ajar. He was quiet and wouldn't even look my way. I walked over to the chair where he was seated and knelt beside him. "You know, I had a nice time," I said. "I wish I were older, so that way you wouldn't be mad, and would probably see me again."

He didn't say a word; he just sat there as if in deep thought.

"I'm sorry for spoiling your night," l whispered, and kissed him on the cheek. "Good-bye!" I rose and started for the door.

"Sugar."

I turned to face him. "Yes?"

He stood up and took a deep breath. "Well." He paused. "Well, good-bye."

I may have been young, but being female, I realized that he wanted to say more.

I gave him a half smile. "Okay." When I turned around, I found the same lady from last night standing in the doorway.

"Oh, are you leaving so soon?" she said sarcastically. "I didn't mean to crash the party."

I could have pulled her hair out by the roots, but I didnít want to give her the satisfaction of thinking that she had defeated me. "Don't worry, baby, you didn't crash it," I said, and gave a sly grin, and added, "The party was last night. He's just waiting for the clean-up woman." I walked out. For some reason when she entered the room, and I heard the door close, a vast emptiness covered me.

Robert was the only one of them giving us a ride. The other two were in the other car. We were sitting in the car, while Robert stood outside talking to his friends.

Joyce was seated in the back next to me. "Girl, what's wrong with you?" she asked. "That man must have really put something on you."

He had, and I didn't feel like joking about it. Without saying a word, I turned my head and looked out the window.

"Don't worry, you'll soon be over it," Laurel said.

I began thinking about how Mom used to tell me to go for what I wanted and don't let nothing or no one stand in my way. He was what I wanted, and I couldn't see that woman standing in my way. Granted, she was older but that really didn't make a difference. I knew I did everything right last night and I made him feel like a man. The look in his eyes when I was leaving told me that he wanted to call me back. I just knew he did, but that woman walked up.

Robert got in the car and started it.

"Wait!" I shouted. Everyone looked at me, as if I were crazy, but I had to do what had been instilled in me, and go for what I wanted. "I'll walk!" I said. "Because I have something I must do."

Joyce knew what was up. As I opened the door, she winked at me. "That's a girl. I know exactly how you feel," she said.

I smiled and stepped outside. Watching the car drive off, and after last night, I felt like a complete woman.

While on the elevator, for some reason I felt confident that he wouldn't object to my returning. I didn't care what the lady thought, because her desires weren't important to me.

I didn't hesitate once I approached the door. I knocked and stood with pride.

The lady answered the door. "Oh, the little girl is back," she said. "I'll tell him you're here."

"No, that's all right. I'll tell him myself." I pushed the door open and walked in.

Tony was lying across the bed on his stomach until he heard us. He was starting to get up and turned to face me.

She literally slammed the door, stormed over, and stood by his side.

"Tony, are you going to ask this baby to leave, or what?" She whined like a spoiled brat.

He stood there staring at me without saying a word. It was a pleasant stare, but yet I still became nervous. He moved closer to me, gazing into my eyes.

The lady became angrier, grabbed his arm, and turned him to face her.

"I asked you to have her leave!" she said.

"No," he said politely, and turned back to face me.

I became weak from his words, as much as from the way he was looking at me.

"What do you mean 'no'?" she butted in again.

"Just as I said." He turned to her. "No!" He took a step closer to her. "In fact, I am going to have to ask you to leave," he told her.

"Me?" she asked, surprised. "What about our plans?"

"What about them?" he said, and turned back to me, and continued, "If it wasn't for this young lady, my coming back to town sure wouldn't have been worth the bother."

"Do you know what you're saying?" she squeaked, now almost in tears.

"Do you know what I'm saying?" he asked. "It's not going to work. We could never get back together because you, my dear, are a nag. I don't have to put up with your snobbish ways any longer." He walked over and opened the door for her.

She looked at me with her eyes full of tears. I stepped to the side and let her stomp past me and out of the door.

He closed the door, and came over and took me in his arms. "Why did you come back?" he asked.

"I don't know. I just had to."

"I'm glad you did. You made me feel alive last night. I came back here to try and get back with her, but you showed me how to live, you made me smile."

After that, Tony got a job at a printing shop as a typesetter

When I turned eighteen, Mother didn't disapprove of Tony and me getting an apartment two miles from her. She just gave me those same words of advice: "Go for what you want!"

THE END

SHE'S A SINGLE MOM–
HE'S A CONVICTED FELON
A remarkable story of enduring love and an ongoing struggle for peace, compassion, and closure

To hear Quincy tell it, her husband is some sort of a modern-day superhero. He is brave and strong and kind; he is an exemplary lover and a judicious father. In Quincy's eyes, her husband is everything a man should be.

The truth?

I'm not any of those things.

Not even close.

I have never been what a person would call "strong." I get scared sometimes and when I'm scared my gut instinct is to run away from my fears. That's where I was when I met Quincy—running scared. In my heart, I know that I would not even be alive today if not for that amazing woman who would not stop believing in me. So if a hero figures anywhere into this equation, Quincy would be that hero. I really have to hand it to her—

Loving me has not been easy.

Eight years ago while out drinking in a bar, I picked up an underage girl and took her to a hotel room. That indiscretion cost me five years of my life. When my prison term ended, the justice system considered my debt to society paid in full, but as far as society is concerned, I will never be done paying for my crime. Because they love me, Quincy and her son, Colin, will pay, too. It's not fair, but that's the way it is.

People can be brutal when they think they know the truth.

I fell in love with Quincy the first time I met her. When I walked into her restaurant, Java Jungle, I was a man without a prayer. Prison did a number on me—body and soul—and I'd just recently completed my rehab program in the psychiatric ward at County General. As a favor to my counselor, Jeff Boettcher, Quincy went out on a limb and hired me as a cook.

She's a beautiful woman—there's no doubt about that—but Quincy's a hell of a lot more than just another pretty face. She's my inspiration. Working side by side with her every day I watched her struggle to run a business while at the same time, be both mother and father to her son. Never once did I see that beautiful smile of hers slip.

When she interviewed me, I told her right upfront that I'd been in prison. I didn't tell her why and she was kind enough not to ask.

As it was, I never wanted Quincy to find out the truth, but of course, with a secret like mine, I knew it was only a matter of time. The day she found out about my sex offender status and came knocking on the door of the motel room where I was living, I thought for certain that she was coming to send me packing. In fact, I was so sure of it that I was already in the process of packing my bags.

She came through the door, saw my open suitcase on the bed, and accused me of running away.

"It won't be good for you if I stay, believe me," I told her. "This relationship isn't going anywhere but down, Quincy, so please—just leave before I do you any more damage." That was an indescribably tough thing for me to say, considering how my heart was breaking at the time.

"I'm not leaving here until you tell me the truth, Tanner," she said. "All of it."

And so, with nothing left to lose—I told her everything. About how my girlfriend, Olivia, dumped me and I went out to a bar looking for solace and found a whole lot of trouble instead. How I picked up a sixteen-year-old girl, thinking she was twenty-five, and took her to a hotel room. Later, the girl accused me of raping her. As quickly as a jury could say guilty, I was branded a convicted sex offender for the remainder of my life.

"This isn't a very big town, Quincy," I told her. "And Colin's school already knows about me, and it's only a matter of time until everyone else knows, too."

"But we know the truth, Tanner!" she said. "How can you give up so easily?"

Once more I tried to send her away. Instead of leaving, she wrapped her arms around me and told me that she loved me.

I held onto her with everything I had because in all honesty, that little girl was the only thing in this world that I had to hold onto. She held me like a lover, and like a mother, murmuring softly that everything would be all right. I wanted to believe it; oh, how I wanted to. But I learned the hard way that life can deal out some pretty lousy cards. As it was, I'd spent the last six years on edge, my nerves frayed, always waiting to be dealt the next losing hand.

Over the weeks that followed, with Quincy's love and her incredible sense of optimism, she finally convinced me. Her faith in me was astounding. Even knowing that I'm on record as a convicted sex offender, she actually wanted to share my life, my name. We got married in a little gazebo in the village square three months later with only Colin, the judge, and a family of curious squirrels as our witnesses.

We spent our honeymoon in a little cabin on Lake Porter: Colin,

Quincy, and me. We swam and played miniature golf and toasted marshmallows over a campfire. As each glorious day melted into the next I started to believe that Quincy was right—that things really would turn out okay for all of us. But as soon as we arrived back home reality crashed into my beautiful daydream. As soon as we pulled into the driveway, I knew that Quincy had made a terrible, terrible mistake by marrying me.

"Oh, dude—look!" Colin shouted as we pulled in. "Someone messed up our house, bad!"

In a panic, I looked over and saw that Quincy's face was a mask of shocked disbelief as she let out a strangled little cry. "Oh, my God!"

Every window in the house was smashed and the words, GET OUT OF TOWN, BABY RAPER! were spray-painted across the front in neon red. Inside, we discovered rocks strewn all over the living room. Rubber-banded to those rocks were scraps of paper with words like CHILD MOLESTER and FREAK scribbled on them.

I stood in the center of the room, dazedly assessing the damage.

"It doesn't mean anything, Tanner," Quincy said gently, wrapping her arms around me. "We'll get through it."

But despite her brave words, I could see that she was trying hard not to cry.

As it turned out, the damage was not just limited to our home. While we were away, Java Jungle was also vandalized. Quincy picked up the phone and called the police, who came over to make out a report. They hadn't been gone even an hour before Quincy's sister, Chelsea, was at our front door.

"You got off easy, girl," she told Quincy, angrily sweeping her hand to indicate the wreckage of our home. "Just wait until you get a look at the restaurant!"

Quincy took a deep breath and then asked, "How bad is it?"

"Oh, it's bad, little sister. The front window's smashed out and there were nasty words spray-painted all over the storefront; I had Tommy Rivard whitewash them, but now the whole building's going to have to be repainted. The cheapest quote I could get was twelve hundred dollars. What I want to know is—who's going to pay for it?"

"Calm down, Chelsea," Quincy said irritably. "I'm sure our insurance policy covers acts of vandalism."

"Yeah, well—there's no insurance policy in the world that's going to rebuild our reputation, now, is there?" She jerked her thumb in my direction. "I want him out, Quincy."

Chelsea never liked me, even from the start. To be honest, the feeling is mutual. But though I find her personality to be as abrasive as a scouring pad, I have to admit—I could see her side. I was a liability; it was just as simple as that.

"I'm sorry, Chelsea," I said. "I truly am."

Quincy turned to Colin, who was watching this entire scene unfold and looking pretty upset. "Colin, go upstairs and unpack your bags."

He hesitated, looking from his mother, to his aunt, to me.

"Go on, now, honey," Quincy coaxed. "And be careful you don't step on any broken glass."

When Colin was safely out of earshot Quincy turned on her sister. "Let's get one thing straight, Chelsea: You and I are equal partners. Fifty/fifty. I have just as much say as you do about how our business runs and I say that my husband stays."

"Here's a clue for you, Quincy!" Chelsea said hotly. "The summer tourists are in town. This should be our peak season and business has never been worse!"

"What do you want me to say?"

"I want you to tell me that you'll sell me your half of Java Jungle."

"No way, Chelsea. Absolutely not. Never in a million years!"

"Just think about me for a minute here, Quincy. Think about our family name. That restaurant has been a respected business in this town for over fifty years and you want to throw all of that away just because of some—"

She stopped herself just in time, but the word she meant to say festered in the air around us like a cancer cell. It was a word I'd been hearing for the last eight years. A word I hated.

Pervert, I silently finished her sentence.

"Get out!" Quincy shouted at her sister.

"I'm only saying that I—"

"Get out!"

Chelsea tried to stare her down, but even she's smart enough to know when it's dangerous to push Quincy's buttons. She walked to the door and then turned back to face us. "This isn't over, Sis," she hissed. "Not by a damn sight!"

Quincy and I talked about it all night. I wanted her to accept Chelsea's offer, thinking that with the money she would get for her half of the business, we could move out of town—or maybe even out of the country. Heck, by that time—I was willing to move to the moon because like I said, since my time in prison, whenever things got ugly my basic survival instinct urged me to put my head down and flee. The only problem was—Quincy refused to budge.

"You don't understand, Tanner!" she cried. "You grew up white in a high-class neighborhood! I grew up half-black in a white man's town! All my life I've had to fight for everything I ever had! I grew up in that restaurant, Tanner, and there's no way in hell that I'm going to be forced out of it now!"

And so Quincy held her head high and stayed on at Java Jungle,

66

but I stood firm in my own decision to bow out gracefully and resigned as cook.

I had some pretty dark days after that. Depression settled over me like a thick, dark fog and some days, it was all I could do just to get out of bed in the morning. Being a househusband takes some getting used to, believe me. I spent my days cooking, cleaning, and doing the wash—not exactly a boost for my already bruised and fast-fading ego. The arrangement did have its upside, though, and that was that I got to spend a lot of time with Colin. At the time, he was coming up fast on thirteen, which is a tough age for any kid. I know that better than anybody.

As Quincy pointed out, I grew up in a wealthy family, but that didn't guarantee me a happy childhood. At thirteen, I was lonely and sad most of the time. A disappointment to my father and swallowed up by the shadows of my superstar brothers, I would've given anything at that age to have someone—anyone at all—in my corner. I sensed that same kind of loneliness in Colin and I wanted so badly to be that someone for my stepson.

So I read all of Quincy's parenting books and then formulated my game plan for fatherhood. I limited Colin's TV time to an hour a day and assigned him some household chores to teach him about responsibility. After his daily chores were done we read books or put together model airplanes or jigsaw puzzles. At that time, I didn't go outside much because it seemed like everywhere I went, there was always someone with something nasty to say to me. I'd replaced the broken windows and affixed motion-sensor lights to the front of the house and though there were no more repeats of vandalism, it was pretty clear that I wasn't going to be considered an accepted member of the community anytime soon. As it was, one by one our neighbors started moving away until our already quiet street began to resemble a ghost town. Even so, Colin and I had a great summer together and I started to think of him as my own son, my flesh and blood.

In September when the first day of school rolled around, I missed him like crazy. I decided to surprise him with his favorite treat, M&M cookies. By three o'clock that afternoon I was watching out the living room window for him to come home, anxious to hear about his first day back at school. But when he walked in the front door at three-fifteen, instead of filling me in, he went straight to his bedroom.

Seeing that he wanted some space, I waited for half an hour and then I piled a plate with cookies and carried them upstairs to his room with a bottle of Yoo-hoo.

"Hey, buddy. How was your first official day as a seventh-grader?" I asked, setting the cookies and Yoo-hoo on his nightstand.

He shrugged. "It was okay."

"You sure about that?"

He shrugged again, making no move toward the cookies or the Yoo-hoo.

"How do you like your new teachers?"

"They're okay."

I knew I shouldn't drill him, but I was starting to get a real uneasy feeling. "Did you make any new friends today?"

That time he didn't answer me at all. He lay down on his bed and turned his face to the wall and I could see that he was struggling to hold back tears.

"What's wrong, dude?" I asked.

"Nothing."

I rested my hand on his shoulder and he recoiled from my touch.

"Hey, buddy—let's talk about it, whatever it is. Let's talk about it, dude to dude."

"They said bad things," he blurted out. "About you."

I felt a tight fist squeeze around my stomach. "What kinds of things?"

"They said you went to bed with a little girl."

"We talked about that, though, didn't we, Col?"

He nodded, but didn't turn over to face me.

"Colin, you're probably going to hear a lot of bad things about me before you're through, but I'm telling you the truth now—just like I've always told you the truth. I never hurt anybody—especially not a child. Okay?"

"Okay."

But I knew it wasn't okay. Far from it.

"Is there anything else you want to ask me about? Anything that was said that's still bothering you?"

"No." He turned over to face me and scrubbed at the tears he could no longer hold back. "Can you go now, Tanner? I want to listen to my music."

I left his after-school snack on the nightstand and walked out of his room feeling discouraged and utterly beaten. Looking in Colin's eyes, I saw how selfish I was, wanting to hold onto what was good for me at any cost and hurting a little dude I cared about in the process.

That night I tried once again to persuade Quincy to sell the house and leave town with me.

"That's not happening, Tanner," she said. "We're not going to let a few narrow-minded people push us out of our own home. We're not going to let them win."

"But what about Colin? Do you really think this is healthy for him?"

"Colin will be all right. Kids have always picked on him, Tanner; this just gives them some new material."

After that day I did everything I could think of to try to make it up to Colin. I planned special outings for just the two of us on the weekends, hoping to recapture some of the ground I'd lost with him; we went to a monster truck show and an NFL game. Colin had recently become interested in wrestling so when W.W.E. came around I even took him to the city to see the show. He never said anything more about what was going on at school, but I could tell by the downcast way he carried himself that things were not getting any easier for him. Then in early October, just when I was feeling like a complete failure as a parent, life handed us a miracle. The For Sale sign disappeared from the yard of the house next door to us.

A few days later Colin and I watched from behind the living room curtains as our new neighbors moved in. The owners appeared to be about the same age as Quincy and I and to Colin's utter delight, we saw a son who looked about his age.

"Dude!" he said excitedly, peering from his place at the window. "He must like to skateboard, too, because I just saw him carry a sweet-looking board inside!"

When Quincy came home from work that afternoon and found Colin and me staked out in front of the window, she scolded us good-naturedly. "Just what are the two of you up to—gawking out the window like a couple of peeping Toms?"

"We're spying on our new neighbors," I said, gathering her in my arms for a kiss. "After all, what else can we do?"

"For starters, we can all go over there and introduce ourselves."

The initial icebreaking went pretty smoothly. Though they obviously had more money than we did, David and Elisa Wallace seemed like decent, down-to-earth people, so the following Saturday we threw some hotdogs and hamburgers on the grill and invited our new neighbors to join us for a cookout. It turned out that David, a computer programmer, and Elisa, an attorney, moved away from the city to our small town to escape the traffic and the escalating crime rate.

"We wanted a safe, quiet place for Evan to grow up," Elisa explained.

Her words tied my stomach in knots as I wondered, What would they think if they knew that a registered sex offender's living just a stone's throw away?

Despite my anxiety, the four of us really clicked together. While Colin and Evan raced off to Colin's room with his newest PlayStation game, David and Elisa and Quincy and I hung out in our family room, talking. Even with our spirited conversation and good-natured kidding, after awhile I felt apprehension creeping around inside of my gut. Quincy and I had decided to tell our new friends the plain truth ourselves before they heard a pack of lies from someone else and so, when there was finally a lull in the conversation, I poured another round of drinks for everyone and told David and Elisa about my situation.

They didn't say anything for what seemed like a very long time after I'd said my piece. Then Elisa finally spoke up. "Well, we certainly appreciate your honesty, Tanner."

Her words were sincere, but right away I felt the atmosphere in the room cool off. Then, after what they must've considered to be a polite interval, Elisa set aside her wineglass and stood. "We should go, hon," she told David. "We still have a million and one things to do. Quincy, thanks so much for inviting us." She turned to me, and her handshake was barely a graze of my hand. "It was nice to meet you, Tanner."

I shook hands with David, as well, and then Quincy called the boys downstairs from Colin's room.

"Aw, they don't have to go now, do they?" Colin whined. "We haven't even beaten the third level yet! Besides, I was gonna invite Evan to spend the night!"

"Please, Mom?" Evan coaxed his mother.

I waited, steeling myself for the onslaught of embarrassed excuses. Well, Tanner, I thought, you let the kid down again. No way are these respected businesspeople going to let their son spend the night under the same roof with a sex offender.

To my infinite surprise, though, Elisa answered, "Well, that would be up to Mr. and Mrs. Berkeley, now, wouldn't it?"

Evan ended up spending the night and just as easily as that, Colin had a new best friend. From then on, the boys walked to and from school together, skateboarded almost incessantly, and spent hours in Colin's room trading wrestling cards. Evan even persuaded Colin to join the wrestling team at school and soon, the hunted look disappeared from Colin's eyes and Quincy and I finally breathed little sighs of relief. But like clockwork, just when things started to settle down for us—

Life dealt us another ugly card.

In early December when we'd been a family for only six months, Quincy's ex-husband called from Nevada to inform her that he intended to fight her for custody of Colin.

I stood beside her in the kitchen, listening to her end of the conversation and trying to put the pieces together.

"But you abandoned him, Joel! . . . Oh, I don't think so . . . He is not! He's a fine, decent man who happens to have spent more time with your son in six months than you have in thirteen years! . . . Fine. Fine! Then I'll see you in court!"

She slammed down the phone and crumpled against me, shaking

from head to toe and crying like her heart would never heal. I'm not a violent man, but I believe if Joel Jackson were standing in our kitchen that night, I would've killed him.

"Oh, Tanner!" Quincy sobbed. "He says he's going to take Colin away from me! He can't do that, can he?"

"No, Quincy, he can't," I said, gently stroking her hair. "And if I'm the reason why he's going to try, then I'll leave."

"You're not going anywhere!" she cried vehemently, wrapping her arms more tightly around me.

"Quincy, sweetheart . . . listen to me. I love you more than life itself; you know that. But I've cost you too much already. I can't let you sacrifice your child for me."

"But you can't leave, Tanner! I'm—"

"I'm tired of messing up your life. The destruction of your home, the rumors and the ugliness—haven't you had enough already, Quincy?"

"You can't leave me, Tanner! You love me too much!" she cried, and then added quietly, her beautiful face alive with feeling, "And besides—we're—we're going to have a baby!"

I pulled away from her and stared into her eyes. "What did you just say?"

"I said . . . we're going to have a baby, Tanner. I was going to tell you after my ob/gyn appointment tomorrow, when it will be official."

"Oh, Quincy." I sighed. "How—how sure are you?"

"Only about ninety-nine-point-nine percent."

I'm ashamed to admit to you that my first reaction was despair. With a newborn in the picture, I realized that Quincy would be saddled with me for the rest of her life. Me, I thought miserably. A failure as a man, as a husband, and already as a father to Colin. How could Quincy possibly bear up under the burden of another child?

But as the days and weeks passed, I started to realize that I was actually happy about the baby. That fragile, little life growing inside of Quincy gave my own sorry life a whole new purpose. I put a fresh coat of pale-yellow paint on the walls of our spare bedroom; I bought a secondhand cradle at an antique shop and spent hours down in our basement, refinishing it. Quincy and I devoured baby-name books, and I went to all of her prenatal appointments with her because I wanted to know everything that was going on with our baby. Most important, I pulled myself together enough to get a job.

I sent some samples of my work to a big-name textbook publisher and was hired the following week to write junior high-level math curriculum. I worked from home, so I still had time and energy to be there for Colin, though with Evan next door he really didn't seem to need me as much, a realization that made the new baby all the more important to me. The day Quincy's doctor found our baby's heartbeat, I was so overwhelmed with joy that I actually broke down and cried.

"It's almost like I can feel it, Quince," I told her, laying my hand across my heart. "Right here."

Quincy gave me one of her million-dollar smiles. "A person would think you're the one who's pregnant!"

"Well, now," I said, chuckling, "that would really give them something to talk about, wouldn't it?"

In the months while we awaited the birth of our child the only thing marring our happiness was our upcoming court date. It stared at us from its blackened box on the calendar, casting a long, dark shadow across our joy. We hired Elisa to represent us and though she assured us that Joel didn't have a legal leg to stand on, I couldn't seem to quiet the nagging doubts that screamed inside my head, telling me that Quincy was going to lose her son and it would be all my fault.

Finally, the date we'd circled in black arrived. Walking into that courtroom I was as nervous as hell, trying not to remember that the last time I'd entered a courtroom, I left in handcuffs. Elisa pleaded our case like a champ, but still, I was uneasy when the judge called Colin into his chambers. Quincy and I sat holding hands, not saying anything, but the way she gripped my hand told me that her nerves were stretched as tautly as mine. What seemed like hours later, the judge and Colin finally reappeared in the courtroom.

"I'm going to tell you all right now, I'm not a bit comfortable with this situation," the judge said, his eyes bearing down on me. "But the child wishes to remain in his home with his mother and his stepfather, and since I see no evidence to suggest that that living situation has been damaging to him in any way, and taking into account that his biological father has had virtually no contact with the boy for the past six years, I'm going to grant his wish. Custody remains with the mother."

Colin let out a whoop of joy. He hugged his mother and gave me a high-five while his so-called "father" stormed out of the courtroom without so much as a good-bye. That evening, we took Colin to his favorite restaurant, Smilin' Joe's, to celebrate, and then across the street to Jimmy and Lou's Awesome Arcade. Quincy sat in a nearby chair as the two of us pumped what must've been fifty dollars' worth of quarters into Colin's favorite arcade game, Tekken 3. The fates seemed to be smiling on Colin all the way around that day and he played more skillfully than ever before. Amid the game's flashing lights and madly screaming sirens he gave me another high-five and shouted, "Look, Dad! I got the all-time high score!"

The word slipped from his lips and went straight into my heart. Not dude, that time. Dad.

In that moment I knew that Colin truly was my son, and that he always will be.

As we entered the final days of Quincy's pregnancy, I tried to convince her to slow down, but she insisted on working right up until the very end.

"I can't just sit around here, waiting to go into labor, Tanner. I'd go insane," she explained.

"Well, just promise me that you'll call me at the very first hint of labor. Make that at the first inkling. Will you promise me that?"

"Yes, Tanner." She grinned and winked at me playfully. "I'll call at the first hint of an inkling."

We made a plan to cover all of our bases in case it happened while she was at work. I went over the plan in my head countless times, even rehearsing it in my dreams. So, I should have been calm, cool, and collected five days later when I got that fateful call from Chelsea.

"We're here at the hospital," she said sharply. "Quincy's water broke."

"Are you sure?" I asked moronically.

"Hell, yes, I'm sure! It made a damned mess in my dining room but I guess I'll have to deal with that later. Anyway, you'd better get over here quick, Tanner. This baby's coming like a freight train."

That statement threw me into a panic and all of my carefully laid plans went straight out the window. The confusion that followed was, I'm sure, like something out of a cartoon as I fumbled to pack a bag for Quincy and get myself out the front door. Luckily, I had enough presence of mind to call Elisa and ask her if she could keep an eye on Colin after school.

"Of course I will, Tanner. Oh, gosh—I'm so excited for you and Quincy! Call us later; we'll bring Colin to the hospital to see the new baby."

Her kindness nearly overwhelmed me. "I appreciate that, Elisa," I choked out.

"Hey, no problem. What are friends for?"

I got in my car and raced to the hospital, breaking every speed limit along the way. Walking back into County General, I couldn't help thinking about how much my life had changed; the last time I'd walked through those doors as a newly rehabilitated mental patient, I'd been a broken man. Now, for the first time in my life, I felt absolutely fulfilled.

And all because of Quincy.

Rather than wait for the elevator, I took the stairs up to the third floor. Chelsea met me in the lobby. "You'd better hurry," she said, propelling me toward the birthing room. "This baby's coming, Papa, with or without you!"

I walked into the birthing room where my wife, my sweet Quincy, lay in a hospital bed, her face etched with the pain of labor and her dark curls damp with sweat. To my eyes, she never looked more beautiful.

"How are you doing, baby?" I asked her tenderly, taking her hand as a nurse helped me slip on a sanitary gown over my street clothes.

She answered me with a brave smile. "I'm okay. Now that you're here."

The nurse informed me that second babies tend to come quickly and that Quincy was already well into her labor, so we started the breathing exercises we learned in our childbirth classes, Quincy gripping my hand so hard that I thought it would fracture. I knew she was in agony and I felt powerless to ease her pain, but if there'd been a way to take that suffering from her and bear it myself, I would've gladly done it. As it was, I could only do my best to help her work through the brutal contractions. The whole time I was dizzy and sick to my stomach, scared, and stressed beyond belief. Everything inside of me wanted to run away, but Quincy had always been there for me and it was my turn to be there for her in every way that she needed me.

What followed were probably the toughest hours of my life as I waited for our baby to be born. They say that grown men shouldn't cry, but when the doctor handed me that gorgeous little girl, I don't mind telling you that I cried just like a baby.

"Hey there, Mia," Quincy said, gently taking our daughter from my arms. "Welcome to the world, baby girl."

After what seemed like all too short a time, the doctor whisked Mia off to the nursery to be cleaned up while Quincy settled in for some much-needed rest. The nurses told me that I should go home and get some rest, too, but I couldn't get myself to leave. An hour later, I was sitting beside Quincy's bed, holding our newborn baby girl in my arms, when Jeff Boettcher, my former counselor, walked in.

"I heard a rumor that the stork made a delivery down here," he said quietly.

"This is the happiest day of my life, Jeff, but I don't mind telling you—I'm terrified, buddy."

Jeff smiled. "You're a father now. It all comes with the territory." He pulled back a corner of Mia's tiny swaddling blanket and studied her for a moment. "I've got to hand it to you, pal—you did excellent work."

I couldn't answer him at first. All I could do was stare at my baby, my beautiful little Mia Grace Berkeley. As it was, I'd been sitting there, trying to remember a verse from the Bible I heard somewhere that talks about the sins of a father being visited upon his children. All I could do was pray to God that my little girl would never have to pay for my mistakes—that she would never have any reason to be ashamed of her old man.

"How am I going to live up to this, Jeff?" I asked him, my voice breaking.

"You just do the very best you can, buddy. That's all any father can do."

I looked over at my beautiful wife, asleep on the bed, and back down at the infant child I held in my arms; her fingers were curled around my thumb like gentle chains wrapped around my heart.

In my daughter's tiny hand, I felt the sobering weight of my new responsibilities. In her trusting eyes, I saw a lifetime of second chances stretching out ahead of me, and I saw living proof that life is good. Then I knew that finally, it was time to stop running—time to stop running away. It was time to stand my ground and be the man Quincy believed I was—the man she deserves.

So this is where we are now, still hanging tough. I don't know what the future will hold and I don't pretend to have all the answers, but there's one thing I do know beyond a shadow of a doubt: There is nothing that life can throw our way that, together, the four of us can't handle.

THE END

FAMILY AFFAIR
I Couldn't Resist His Brother

"**H**ow about your digits?" I'd been dancing with Jeryl most of the night, so I wasn't surprised when he asked for my number. I took his cell phone from his outstretched hand and quickly programmed my name and number into it.

The evening had started like most Thursdays. The club did not serve liquor to the under-21 crowd on teen night, but we all managed to enjoy ourselves anyhow, dancing in one of the three cavernous rooms.

Earlier that evening, Jeryl had approached me in the Urban Room, where the music was mostly hip-hop and rap, and we had been dancing together ever since. We'd tried to talk, but the music was too loud, and we barely knew anything about each other by the time the DJ announced the last dance.

I had hoped to learn more about Jeryl after I returned his cell phone, but one of his friends grabbed his arm and pulled him away.

"I have to bounce," he called over his shoulder. "I'll hit you up later."

Marla found me outside, standing next to her car.

"Where have you been all night?" she asked. "I thought we were going to the Karaoke Room. I waited for you."

"I was dancing."

"With who?"

I told her about Jeryl as we climbed into her car and she keyed the ignition.

"That's all you know about him?" she asked.

"I know he can dance," I said. "And you know what it means if a guy can dance."

Marla shook her head. "Is that all you think about?"

"That and food," I said. "Let's stop for burgers before we return to the dorm."

Later turned out to be Saturday afternoon. I was walking through the mall with Marla when my cell phone rang. Even though I didn't recognize the number, I answered.

Jeryl identified himself.

As soon as I realized who it was, I stopped Marla and mouthed, "It's him."

"Him, who?" she asked.

I mouthed, "From last night."

"Me and some friends are going to Sylvester's tonight," Jeryl said. "You want to meet us there?"

"What time?"

We worked out the arrangements and then disconnected. I told Marla about it and asked if she wanted to go with me.

"You won't disappear on me again, will you?"

I assured her that I wouldn't.

That evening, just before nine o'clock, Marla and I walked in the front door of Sylvester's and had the backs of our hands stamped with a giant X because we were underage. Before we made it three steps into the bar, Jeryl slid between us and wrapped his arms around our waists. He guided us to a table where three of his friends sat.

He introduced his friends and I introduced them to Marla. Marla took an instant liking to one of Jeryl's friends, so I didn't have to pay much attention to her for the rest of the evening. Instead, I had a chance to talk with Jeryl. He told me he lived with his parents and younger brother on the other side of town, and I told him that Marla and I shared a dorm room at the college.

"College girls?" Jeryl said. "That's all right."

"What about you? What do you do?"

"A little of this," he said, "and a little of that."

Before I could get him to explain what he meant, Marla grabbed my arm and asked if I needed to use the restroom. I didn't, but I knew she wanted me to join her. We left the guys sitting at the table.

Once we were inside the restroom, Marla asked me what I thought of Mason. I couldn't remember which one he was, but I said, "Yeah, he's cute."

"He wants me to go back to his place."

"You barely know him."

"But he's so hot."

I wasn't sure why Marla wanted my approval. She just wanted me to know that she was about to abandon me.

"Can you get back to the dorm without me?"

"I'll get a ride from Jeryl, I guess."

Marla squeezed my arm. "Good."

She touched up her lipstick, and then we returned to the table. A moment later, she and Mason walked out of the bar together and I was left with Jeryl and his other two friends. He gave them a look and they took the hint. Soon the two of us were alone at the table.

Jeryl put his hand on my thigh under the table and I didn't stop him. In fact, I rather liked it.

We began seeing each other regularly after that, even after Marla and Mason called it quits two weeks after they met. She never did tell me why they stopped seeing each other, but I had the feeling he asked her to do something she wouldn't do.

Since Jeryl lived with his parents and wouldn't take me there, and since I lived in a dorm, there weren't many opportunities to be alone together, but we managed. We hooked up at Mason's apartment a couple of times, and once at a party at one of the sorority houses.

Jeryl wasn't good about making plans, and he always wanted me to be available when he called. I didn't mind, because he was so good looking that Marla and some of my other friends envied me, and when I wasn't with him I was usually just hanging around the dorm.

Before long, I realized Jeryl had a bit of a jealous streak. If I mentioned other guys in front of him--especially if I said anything positive about their looks--his face tightened up and sometimes I even saw a flash of something dark in his eyes. He seemed to be the same kind of guy I'd dated all through high school, the kind of guy my parents had hoped I'd avoid once I went away to college.

I told Marla about it one afternoon while we were eating lunch in the cafeteria.

"You need to be careful," she said. "He might not be all that you think he is."

"It's been three months," I said. "I think I know him pretty well by now."

"Then how come you've never been to his house?" Marla asked. She was all up in my face about my relationship with Jeryl and she just kept throwing questions at me. If I didn't know better, I might have thought she wanted him for herself. "You said he lives just across town. What's he hiding?"

I was still thinking about Marla's question when I met Jeryl at Sylvester's that evening. I asked him about it.

"You really want to meet my family?"

"Yes," I said. "I do."

"How about Saturday?"

Jeryl's parents weren't home when we arrived. His father was at work and his mother was shopping. At first I thought it was just a coincidence, but later I suspected it was on purpose. I don't think he really wanted me to meet his family.

I was surprised when Jeryl introduced his younger bother Deryl, because he had never mentioned that they were twins. He'd always told me he was a year older than Deryl, something he clarified when he told me that he had been born at 11:58 p.m. on December 31 and that Deryl at 12:06 a.m. January 1.

At first, I couldn't tell the two brothers apart. Then I noticed the small scar across the bridge of my boyfriend's nose and Deryl's constantly laughing eyes.

When we were alone in Jeryl's room later, I told him, "Your brother's hot."

Jeryl's face tightened up. "How can you say that?"

"He looks just like you!"

"Stupid bitch!" Jeryl backhanded me across the mouth and I fell backward onto the bed. Then Jeryl turned and stormed out of the room, slamming the door behind him.

I tasted blood inside my mouth, so I gingerly touched my cheek. I'd known that Jeryl had a jealous streak, but jealous of his own brother? That was too much.

A moment later the door opened, and I cringed when I saw Jeryl poke his head into the room. Only it wasn't Jeryl, it was Deryl.

"Are you OK?" he asked. He stepped into the room and quietly closed the door behind him. "I heard what my brother said."

Deryl settled onto the bed next to me and put his arm around my shoulder. "Sometimes my brother can be such a jerk."

I don't know why, but I felt safe in his arms.

"Aren't you afraid that Jeryl will find us like this?"

"He stormed out of the house," Deryl explained. "My brother always does that when he's upset. He won't be back for at least an hour."

"I didn't mean to upset him. I just--"

Deryl touched my chin and turned my face toward him. When I grimaced, he asked, "He hit you, didn't he?"

"He--"

"Has he ever hit you before?"

"No," I said. "Never."

Deryl stood and took my hand. "Come into the bathroom. I'll get you a washcloth and an ice pack."

He made me sit on the toilet seat while he ran cold water over a fresh washcloth. He handed it to me, and then disappeared from the bathroom. He returned a moment later with a baggie filled with ice.

After I wiped off my mouth, I pressed the ice against my cheek.

I was sitting in the living room when Jeryl returned. Before he said anything to me, Deryl grabbed his arm and dragged him into the kitchen. I couldn't hear everything they said, but it was obvious Deryl was chewing out his older brother.

"A girl like that doesn't deserve your bad attitude," Deryl told Jeryl. "Isn't it about time you got your act together and quit treating girls like that?"

Jeryl returned to the living room a few minutes later and grabbed my hand. "We need to get out of here."

"But I haven't met your parents."

"Another time." He dragged me out of the house.

I barely had time to glance back and see Deryl standing in the kitchen door watching us before we were out the front door.

Once we were in Jeryl's car and headed across town toward the college, he mumbled an apology for striking me. When he stopped his car at the curb outside the dorm, he leaned over to kiss me, but I turned my face away and his lips landed on the cheek he hadn't hit.

He took the hint and didn't force the issue. As I climbed out of his car, Jeryl said, "I'll hit you up later."

Somehow, his usual way of saying good-bye no longer seemed appropriate, and I wondered if I was really attracted to his bad boy attitude. I'd always dated guys who expected me to hang on their arms like trophies and it seemed like Jeryl was turning out just like them.

Things changed between Jeryl and I after that. I still dated him, but I didn't quite trust him. Other guys had treated me bad, but none had ever struck me before. We went out twice that week, once for fast food with his friends and once to the dance club, but I was careful not to be alone with him.

And I certainly didn't mention other guys in front of Jeryl, not even his look-alike brother, who I seemed to be thinking a lot about.

I was surprised when Deryl phoned me late Friday afternoon, shortly after I had returned to my dorm room following two hours in the library with classmates working on a group project in Earth Sciences.

"How did you get my digits?" I asked.

"From Jeryl's phone," Deryl explained. "He doesn't know I'm calling."

"So why are you calling?" I asked.

"I want to know if everything is OK."

"Everything's fine," I said, rather too quickly.

"You don't sound like everything's fine."

I didn't say anything.

"I know Jeryl's going out of town for the weekend," Deryl said. He was visiting a friend he'd gone to high school with who had moved away shortly after graduation. "Would it be OK if I took you to dinner?"

"Tonight?"

"I can pick you up whenever you'll be ready."

I hesitated, trying to imagine the consequences of having dinner with my boyfriend's twin brother. Deryl waited patiently until I finally told him he could pick me up in front of my dorm at seven.

Marla arrived a few minutes after our conversation ended and found me changing clothes. She took one look at what I was wearing and asked, "Are you going out tonight?"

"Sort of."

"I thought Jeryl was out of town," she said. "He'll be upset if he finds out you're seeing someone else."

"I'm not 'seeing' someone else," I said. "I'm having dinner with his brother."

Marla cocked her head to one side and stared at me for the longest time. I think she wanted to say something, but couldn't find the right words.

I finished dressing and walked down to the dorm's lobby, where I watched television with a half dozen other students until Deryl arrived promptly at seven.

He took me to an out-of-the-way Chinese restaurant, a place so far off the beaten path that I'm surprised he didn't need a compass and a map to find it. When I asked him why he'd chosen that particular restaurant, he just shrugged.

We talked about inconsequential things--where I grew up and why I'd chosen to attend a college so far from home--until we were nearly finished with our meal. That's when Deryl dropped the bomb on me.

"I've been thinking about you ever since we met last week," Deryl said. "I haven't been able to get you out of my mind."

"But I'm dating your brother," I protested.

"I know," Deryl said. "That's why I thought it was best to wait until I could get you alone to tell you how I felt."

I glanced around. We weren't alone, but we certainly weren't around anybody I knew. "What do you expect from me?"

Deryl shook his head. "I don't know. I just thought you should know how I felt."

I took a deep breath and let it out slowly. Neither of us said anything for the longest time, and we finished our meal in silence.

The waitress brought the check and a pair of fortune cookies. When I opened mine, I found two fortunes inside. The first said, "The heart knows what it wants." The second said, "True love is within your grasp."

Deryl read his fortune to me--"Shared secrets are no longer secret."--and then asked what mine said.

"It's not important," I told him. Then I crumpled my fortunes up and dropped them into my iced tea glass.

Deryl stared deep into my eyes for a moment, as if trying to read my thoughts. Then he paid for our meal and walked me to his car. After he unlocked the door, he turned to face me.

We were alone in the parking lot, and a cool breeze threaded through the cars to send a slight chill racing up my spine. A full moon hung in the sky above us, and for a moment everything was quiet.

Deryl leaned forward and kissed me. I wasn't expecting it, but I didn't resist. His lips were soft and his kiss was tender, sending a warm shiver racing down my spine. His brother's kisses had never been like this.

81

I wrapped my arms around Deryl and pulled him forward until his muscular body trapped mine against his car. The kiss lengthened and deepened. I closed my eyes and let the moment wash over me. My heart began to beat wildly in my chest and my knees turned to rubber.

When the kiss finally ended and Deryl pulled away, I could barely stand. I looked up at him and said, "You'd better take me back to the dorm."

We rode across town in silence and I stared out the passenger window, afraid to even glance at my boyfriend's twin brother because I couldn't understand all the conflicting feelings I had racing through me.

When Deryl finally pulled his car to the curb in front of the dorm, I opened my door and slipped out. I knew I had to say something, so I leaned back in and said, "Thanks for dinner."

Then I closed the car door and hurried into the dorm. I didn't look back until I was inside the building, safely behind the glass doors. That's when Deryl finally pulled away from the curb, and I watched his car's taillights until they disappeared around the corner two blocks away.

Marla had been lying on her bed reading a play for her British Lit class. As soon as I entered our room, she rolled over and asked, "So?"

"It was just dinner," I told her, and then I tried to change the subject. "Why aren't you out tonight?"

She didn't take the bait. Instead she sat up and asked, "If it was just dinner, then why's your lipstick smeared?"

My hand instantly went to my face, and I felt lipstick on my cheek.

"You're in dangerous territory," she said. "It's hard enough to date two guys, but dating brothers is going to be impossible."

"I'm not dating both of them," I insisted. "I'm dating Jeryl."

"So you're dating Jeryl and just making out with his brother," Marla said. "Is that it?"

"That's not it," I insisted. "That's not it at all."

"Methinks you protest too much," Marla said, and I realized she was reading Shakespeare.

I turned around and left the room. I walked to the communal bathroom and washed my face, removing all of my makeup. When I returned to the room, Marla was reading again, and I didn't interrupt her. Instead, I changed into my favorite pajamas and put myself to bed, pulling the covers over my head to block out the light.

I tossed and turned all night, never quite getting comfortable because I found myself dreaming about Jeryl and Deryl. Sometimes I could tell them apart in my dreams and sometimes I couldn't. When I woke the next morning, I felt just as conflicted as I had before going to bed.

Things didn't get any better when my cell phone rang and it was Jeryl telling me about the concert he'd gone to the night before. He spent the entire conversation talking about himself and his friend and never once asked how I was doing or what I was doing. He finally ended the conversation by saying, "I'll hit you up later."

When Jeryl hung up, I realized I had a message waiting. I hit the button to play the message and heard Deryl's voice. "I'll be at Big Momma's at noon. Meet me there if you're hungry."

Big Momma's is a hamburger joint just across the street from campus, a place where a lot of college students eat when they get fed-up with cafeteria food but don't want to travel far.

I squinted at the clock and realized I had plenty of time to get ready if I decided I wanted to meet Deryl. Marla had disappeared before I woke up, so I had the room to myself. I did some homework, straightened up my side of the room, and then took a long, hot shower in the communal bathroom.

At 11:45 I headed across campus, arriving at Big Momma's a few minutes before noon. Deryl was already there, seated in one of the booths by the front door. He stood when he saw me.

"I wasn't sure you'd come," he said.

"I wasn't sure either, until a few minutes ago," I told him, even though I'd made up my mind before I'd ever gotten in the shower.

We sat and a few minutes later Big Momma herself came to take our order. She took one look at us and said, "Y'all want the Lovebird Special?"

I looked up in surprise, but Deryl asked, "What's the Lovebird Special?"

"One malt, two straws, just like in them old-time movies."

"No, thank you," I told her.

"Suit yourself, young'uns, but y'all be ordering one before too much longer."

We told her what we wanted--grilled chicken salad for me, a bacon cheeseburger for Deryl, and a cola for each of us--and then she left us to take our order to the kitchen.

"What was that all about?" I asked once Deryl and I were alone at the table.

He shrugged. "She's just being friendly."

Before I could say anything else, Marla walked through the front door, spotted us, and walked directly to our table. She looked hard at Deryl for a minute, and then asked, "Which one is this?"

I introduced her to Deryl.

"Smooth," she said, "moving in on your brother's girl."

"It's not like that," Deryl protested.

Marla looked at me, and then turned her back. She crossed the restaurant and joined a table where three girls from our dorm already sat.

Marla said something to them and they all looked in our direction.

I ignored them as best I could, but I knew it wouldn't be long before everyone in the dorm knew I was seeing twin brothers.

As soon as we finished eating lunch, I told Deryl to take me someplace away from campus. He drove to the river and we walked hand-in-hand along the riverbank. I felt comfortable with Deryl in a way that I didn't feel comfortable with Jeryl.

We walked and talked for nearly an hour before I realized how far we had gone and suggested that we turn around. Before we did, though, Deryl pulled me into his arms and kissed me.

Just like the night before, his kiss was tender yet passionate, sending liquid desire shooting through my veins. I wanted him in a way that I'd never wanted another guy in my life, not even his look-alike brother.

I pressed myself against him and felt his desire rising. I wondered if he would try to take me right there, along the riverbank, and I wondered if I would even resist.

He didn't though, and soon I was walking rubber-legged back toward the car. Deryl had his arm wrapped around my shoulder and I leaned against him for support.

We talked about all sorts of things as we walked back to the parking lot where we'd left Deryl's car, and Deryl actually listened to what I had to say. As we approached his car I told him how much I appreciated it. Then I told him about his brother's early morning phone call and how Jeryl had never once asked about me.

"My brother's an idiot," Deryl said. "He wouldn't know how to treat a woman right even if she gave him step-by-step instructions."

"And you do?" I asked.

Deryl stopped and turned toward me. He took both of my hands in his and stared deep into my eyes. "I know how to treat you right," he said. "I would never do anything to make you think otherwise."

Deryl and I spent the rest of the day together and most of that night as well. I'd had sex before--his bother hadn't been the first, either--but Deryl taught me what it was like to make love. He used his fingers and his tongue in ways I never could have imagined, and I was practically screaming with desire before he finally consummated the act.

Afterward, I just lay in his arms, fighting to catch my breath and wondering why I had never experienced that overwhelming sense of release with any other guy. Perhaps it was because all the other guys were self-centered, more concerned with pleasing themselves than anything else. Even though I'd known it before we slept together, the time we spent in bed confirmed what I knew. Deryl was special in more ways than I could begin to understand.

As I stared at the ceiling and listened to Deryl's heartbeat, I realized I was cheating on my boyfriend with his brother--his twin brother--and somehow I didn't feel the least bit guilty about it. Jeryl had never treated me as well as Deryl did, and probably never would.

I had to tell my boyfriend the truth.

Jeryl returned from his trip the following afternoon and phoned me. He wanted to see me that evening, so I told him we could meet at Big Momma's for dinner.

Then I phoned Deryl.

"I have to tell him," I said, not realizing that Marla was standing in the hallway listening to everything I said. "It wouldn't be right not to, but I'm afraid of Jeryl's temper. That's why I told him we'd meet in a public place."

"Don't worry," Deryl said. "I'll come with him."

"How will you manage that?"

"I'll think of a way," Deryl said, his calm voice reassuring me.

I spent the rest of the afternoon nearly out of my head with worry, but true to his word, Deryl arrived at the restaurant with Jeryl. Jeryl slipped into the booth beside me, trapping me against the window, and Deryl sat across the table from me.

Although I didn't realize she was there until later, Marla sat in the booth behind me with a couple of the other girls from our dorm.

"I've missed you, baby," Jeryl said. He leaned over to kiss me and I turned my face just in time. His kiss landed on my cheek. "I've been thinking about you the entire way home."

"Did you think about me at all while you were gone?" I asked.

"I called you, didn't I?"

"You called to tell me what a good time you were having," I said. "You didn't ask about me at all."

"It's no biggie," Jeryl said. He put one hand on my thigh under the table and squeezed. "I'm back now."

I took a deep breath and pushed his hand away. "I'm seeing someone else."

Jeryl looked surprised. "Who?"

Despite my best effort not to, I glanced at Deryl. "It isn't important," I said. "What's important is that I realized he's the one for me."

"That's bullshit!" Jeryl said.

I tried to calm him down. I put a hand on Jeryl's forearm, but he shook it off.

"It isn't you," I said. "It's nothing you did."

That's when Marla leaned over the back of the booth and said, "It's your brother."

Jeryl spun around to look at Marla, and then he spun back to glare at Deryl.

"You just want her because I have her," he said to Deryl. "You try to take everything I have."

I hadn't thought of that. I looked at Deryl. "Is that true?"

Deryl denied it. "It's not like that at all."

"It better not be," I told him.

Jeryl turned back to me. "Deryl always wants whatever I have."

"And he's had her, all right," Marla said.

I told her to shut up and stay out of it.

"Hey, you picked a public place to dump your boyfriend," she said. "You get what you deserve."

The girls at her table laughed.

Jeryl shoved himself out of the booth. "You want her," he shouted at his brother. "You can have her. I'm done with this trash."

Jeryl stormed out of Big Momma's, leaving Deryl and I staring at each other. A moment later, his car's tire squealed against the asphalt as his car shot out of the parking lot.

Marla was still leaning over the back of the booth. "You sure you picked the right one? Looks like the smart one is I spun around to face her. "Oh, shut up!"

Then I slid out of the booth and stormed out of the restaurant myself, with Deryl only a few steps behind me. He caught my elbow in the parking lot and slowed me down.

Then he took me in his arms and held me while I started to cry.

"It wasn't supposed to be like this," I said.

Deryl brushed my hair away from my face when I looked up at him and everything seemed to be OK.

Everything was crazy for the next few days. Jeryl left messages on my cell phone, a combination of insults and accusations that often ended with pleas for me to give him a second chance. He said he knew he could give me anything his brother could give me.

I had an argument with Marla that didn't end until the Resident Advisor assigned me to a different dorm room two floors below my old room, and I found myself sharing space with a girl who barely spoke two words to anyone.

Then Jeryl stopped leaving messages and things seemed to return to normal. Two weeks later, Deryl told me Jeryl had moved out of their parents' house.

"He moved in with his friend up north," Deryl explained, "the one he was visiting the weekend we got together. He said he doesn't want to risk running into you around town. He said you broke his heart and he'll never forgive you for that."

"If he really cared about me, he would have treated me better," I said.

"He stills thinks I stole you away on purpose."

"Did you?"

"Yes," Deryl said, "but not for the reason he thinks. I fell in love with you the moment I met you. The funny thing is, I have you now and I still can't stop thinking about you. I wake up thinking about you and I fall asleep thinking about you. Imagine what my life would have been like if I hadn't stolen you away from my brother."

I stretched up and kissed my boyfriend. The fortunes I'd received in my fortune cookie the first time Deryl and I had gone out were right: the heart does know what it wants and true love was within my grasp.

THE END

PARTY GIRL
She's Not The Right Woman For My Son

No mother wants her child to be lonely, even when the child is a thirty-seven-year-old man. My heart broke each time Josh came to drop his three children off at my house so he could go to work. It had been five years since his wife, Benita, had been killed in a car accident and Josh still hadn't moved past his loss.

That's why I was so surprised when he came to Sunday dinner with a young woman named Sasha and announced that they were going to be married. I hadn't even known that he was dating anyone, much less planned to get married. And Sasha was so young. There was only nine years difference between Sasha's age and the age of Jacob, Josh's oldest child.

After the announcement, I did my best to stay composed. "Welcome to our family, Sasha," I said.

"Thank you, Mrs. Vaughn," she answered, giving me a hug.

"Call me Rita," I said.

Sasha smiled as though we were now best friends. "Rita, when Josh and I get married, I hope you'll come over and help me redecorate the house."

"What's wrong with it?" I didn't see the need to change anything. Benita had excellent taste and the house was just fine as it was.

"I want to brighten it up, and give the children a place where they can bring their friends. Jacob's at that age where a boy needs watching and the best way to do it is to have him bring his friends to his house."

"Jacob plays sports after school and on weekends he has games and church."

She continued smiling. "I know, but I want his home to be a place kids can come to after games or practices."

My thoughts turned to Benita and wondered what she'd think about her children being raised by this young woman who wore the shortest skirts I'd ever seen, and a much too revealing shirt.

When Benita died, Jacob was eleven, Tamara was nine, and Angel, the baby, was four. I'd taken care of them, driven them to school, helped them with homework, and seen to it that supper was on the table when Josh got in from work. After dinner Josh would take them home. I wondered when he'd found an opportunity to hook up with Sasha Bennett.

"Let's take our coffee in the living room and you two can tell us all about how you met," I suggested.

Once we were seated, Sasha grew quiet, leaving it up to Josh to handle the details. "We met at a diner where we were both having lunch," Josh said.

I could always tell when my children were lying. And Josh was the worst liar of the bunch. "Which diner?" I asked.

Josh rubbed his chin. I'd caught him in a lie and he knew it. "Can't remember the name. But it's close to where I work."

"Son, the only thing close to where you work is a freight yard, some shady motels, and a few strip clubs," I said. "Sasha, where do you work?"

"She's a maid," Josh answered quickly. "She cleans rooms at one of the motels."

Sasha nodded and that was the end of it because they made an excuse to leave. I tried to talk to Arthur, my husband, after they'd gone, but he wanted to watch a baseball game so he tuned me out. I called Cara, my oldest daughter, and told her about Josh and his new woman.

"Mom, something sounds fishy," she said. "But if he has his mind made up, there's not a thing you can do. Josh is a grown man. Maybe she'll be good for the kids. Give her a chance. She might prove to be a great step-mother."

Cara was right. I had to give Sasha a chance. I went so far as to hold the wedding at our house. It surprised me that no one from Sasha's family came to the wedding. Later she told me her family lived in another state, and that her mother wasn't able to travel.

Right after the wedding things began to change really fast. Josh no longer brought the children to me in the mornings. Sasha got them to school and picked them up. I was lucky if I saw them on weekends.

A few months into the marriage, Josh was offered a job as a driver for the trucking company. It meant more money, but he'd be gone a lot. He'd been offered the job before, but turned it down because of the children. This time he accepted it.

"How can you stand being away from your kids?" I asked him.

"They're older, and they have Sasha now. She'll take care of them. Besides, we need the money."

It was useless for me to argue with him. He'd already accepted the job, and there wasn't a thing I could do besides make a better effort to get to know his wife. I made up my mind that I'd do just that so I baked a cake and took it to the house.

Sasha greeted me at the door wearing a short satin robe. "Oh, Rita, I wasn't expecting you," she said in a sleepy voice.

"I got an urge to bake and went a little overboard," I said. "So I wanted you all to have this cake. It's Josh's favorite."

"How sweet of you. I'm sure we'll love the cake." As an afterthought she added, "Would you like to come in for some coffee?"

"Thank you, that would be nice," I said.

The second I stepped into the living room I was shocked. All of the furniture had been replaced and the walls had been painted a bright yellow. A big screen television sat against one wall, and there were several speakers placed around the room that hooked into an expensive looking CD player.

Right then I realized why Josh needed more money. Sasha had gotten him deeply into debt. "The house looks so different," I said.

"It should. I've spent hours redecorating and getting rid of that depressing old furniture that Josh has had forever."

We went to the kitchen and she made instant coffee. Never, in my entire life, had I ever served a guest instant coffee. I also noticed that the sink was filled with cereal bowls and glasses with the remainder of orange juice in the bottoms. At my house the children had always eaten a hot breakfast.

"Sasha, I'm sorry if I woke you."

"Don't worry about it. I needed to get up early today. I'm redecorating our bedroom and I'm going to look at fabrics."

"How did the children get to school?" I asked.

"Jacob drove them. We bought him a used car from a friend of mine. Got a great deal on it. Jacob drives the kids to school, and I pick them up in the afternoon if he has practice. When he doesn't have practice he brings them home."

"Who fixes their lunches?"

"Tamara is old enough to do it, so I have her make them while Angel gets breakfast on the table. Children need responsibility to help them mature, don't you think?"

She didn't really want to hear what I thought. The very idea of Jacob, who'd just turned sixteen, being given a car and the responsibility of getting his sisters to school was unthinkable.

"I was under the impression that you were going to get them off to school each day," I said. "If it's too much trouble for you, I don't mind doing it. Bring them to my house like Josh used to."

"That wouldn't solve anything," she said, and then yawned. "Rita, I'm a late sleeper. If I get up before ten o'clock I'm useless for the rest of the day. Before I married Josh I used to sleep until one in the afternoon."

How, I wondered, was she able to clean motel rooms if she slept until one in the afternoon? Most maids showed up for work very early so that the rooms would be cleaned before the guests' check-in time.

Sasha covered her mouth as she yawned again. "I can't get used to this new routine. And Josh goes to bed so early. Since we got married we haven't been out at all."

"If you want to get out of the house some, we have bingo at

Church on Thursday nights and I'd be glad to pick you."

She gave me a look like I'd lost my mind. "You're joking, right?" When she realized I was serious she burst out laughing. "I don't do bingo, Rita. I like to go to a place where Josh and I can kick up our heels and have some fun."

As soon as it was polite, I made an excuse to leave. From the look on Sasha's face, she was glad to see me go. We had nothing in common. How a man who'd been married to a woman like Benita could marry someone like Sasha baffled me.

Once I reached my house I called Josh. "You and I are going to have to have a little talk," I said. "Josh, I went to visit your wife today, and there are some things that are troubling me."

"Momma, I love Sasha, and I'm not going to let you bad mouth her to me."

"Did you know that she makes Tamara fix lunch for everybody, and little Angel has to make breakfast? Josh, have you lost your mind letting Jacob have his own car? He doesn't have enough driving experience to be turned loose on the highway. And he's taking the girls to school so your Diva of a wife can sleep late."

"This isn't any of your business. I don't want to hear another word about my wife. I appreciate all that you did for me after Benita died, but now it is time for you to let go."

He slammed the phone down. Josh had never treated me so disrespectfully. What had gotten into him? It was like he'd been bewitched by that awful woman. I told Arthur about what was going on and he suggested I keep my nose out of Josh's affairs.

As hard as it was, I didn't interfere anymore. Josh brought the children to see me every couple of months, and when we had family gatherings, Sasha would come with him, but other than those times, I didn't see or speak to my son's family.

Months had passed when Angel's school counselor called and told me that Angel was sick and asked if I would come get her. Sasha couldn't be reached. Of course I went to the school and picked up my granddaughter. She was so glad to see me that she ran into my arms and hugged me as tightly as she could.

"Oh, Granny, I'm so glad you came. I want to go home with you and I want to stay with you."

"Mrs. Vaughn, Angel has complained of a headache every day for the past two weeks," Miss Ellis, the counselor said. "I've sent home notes, but no one has responded. I think she needs to see a doctor."

"Baby," I said to Angel, "what's wrong?"

"My head hurts, Granny. And I can't see the blackboard. Ms. Tanner moved me to the front desk, but I still can't see."

"Has your daddy taken you to get your eyes examined?" Bad

eyesight ran in the family. Both of my daughters had worn glasses since the age of ten.

"Daddy's never home and Sasha told me I was just trying to get attention. She makes me go to my room and stay there after I eat supper. Tamara and I aren't allowed downstairs at night. Tamara told Daddy but he said Sasha was right. We needed to be in our rooms so we could study instead of watching TV."

"I'm taking you to have your eyes examined," I said. "And then I'm having a talk with your Daddy."

There was an optical shop a few miles from the school that accepted walk-ins so I took Angel there. Sure enough, she was nearsighted and needed glasses. Knowing that she might not get them if I left it up to Sasha, I bought Angel a pair, and then took her home with me.

She asked for a snack, so I served her milk and some cookies I'd baked the day before. I'd never seen her eat so much so fast in her entire life. "Baby, I can make you something else if you're still hungry."

"I'd love some of your fried chicken," she said. "We don't ever have it anymore. Sasha buys stuff that you cook in the microwave. Sometimes she buys pizza when Jacob's friends are there."

"Are Jacob's friends at the house much?" It seemed odd that Sasha would let a bunch of rowdy boys into her newly remodeled house.

"Every day. Sometimes the boys aren't even Jacob's friends. They just come over and hang out with Sasha. She lets them drink beer."

"Does your daddy know that Sasha is letting underage boys drink at your house?"

"She said we'd better not tell him or she'd punish us. Besides, Daddy doesn't believe anything we tell him anyway."

"Well, I believe you." I went to the phone and called Sasha's number. The phone rang several times before a voice I'd never heard answered it.

"Who is this?" I asked.

"Jamal," he said.

"Put Sasha on the phone," I demanded.

"She ain't here." He slammed down the phone.

I called Cara and asked her to come and stay with Angel. No matter who got offended, I was going to find out what was going on in my son's house. I drove over there and parked a block away so Sasha wouldn't see my car and walked to the house, hiding in a neighbor's yard.

Jacob drove into the driveway, his car loaded with boys. I sneaked closer to the house, and the nearer I got the louder the music was. Sasha pulled into the drive. When she got out of the car she went to the trunk and took out two cases of beer which she carried inside.

Laughter, and loud music, could be heard. And no one was laughing louder than Sasha. I wondered where Tamara was, and if she was safe. I gazed up to her bedroom window and saw that there was a light on. I sneaked to the back door and used the spare key Josh had given me. I opened the door that led to the laundry room, and crept up the back stairs. I reached Tamara's room. The door was locked. I knocked lightly.

"Go away and leave me alone," she yelled.

"Baby, it's Granny," I said.

Tamara pulled the door open and I went into her bedroom. She closed and locked the door. "Granny, I'm so glad you're here. I wanted to call you lots of times but I was afraid."

"What's going on in this house?" I asked, dreading the answer.

"It's Sasha. She has young boys coming over here all the time when Daddy's gone. The reason she got a car for Jacob was so he could bring his friends here."

"Why would a grown woman want a rowdy bunch of high school boys hanging out at her house?"

Tamara bit her bottom lip and looked down. Tears streaked her face. "Granny, Sasha has sex with the boys and they pay her. I've seen her go into Jacob's bedroom with more than one boy. She knows that Angel and I know what's going on because she told us if we breathe a word of it she'll let the boys do to us what they do to her. Sasha threatened to invite some men over who'd pay her money to have sex with girls like me and Angel."

"Surely, your father has an idea that something isn't right."

"Daddy said if we don't mind Sasha and do everything she says when he comes home from his trip he'll spank us. She acts so nice when he's home, but when he's gone it's party all the time. Jacob covers for her because she doesn't tell Daddy how bad he's doing in school. Granny, Jacob's failing three subjects.'"

My mind was like a huge fog. How could something like this be going on in my son's house? Why hadn't the neighbors called and complained? The noise would be enough to get the police out there. "Tamara, come with me," I said. "I'm taking you home to my house, and then I'm going to talk to your daddy. He'll have to listen this time."

She wound her thin arms around me and hugged me for all she was worth. "Thank you, Granny."

We sneaked out of the house and ran to my car. I drove us home, and sent Tamara into the kitchen for something to eat while I called Josh.

"Momma, what's wrong?"

"Plenty. Your wife is having orgies with young boys while you're out of town, and she's threatening your daughters that if they tell she'll sell them to men for sex. Josh, I've seen it for myself. And I'm not letting Tamara and Angel back into that house."

"You've blown something out of proportion," he said. "Besides, you can't take the word of a couple of kids over that of a grown woman. I know Sasha. She'd never do what you're suggesting."

"Like I said, I've seen it with my own eyes. I saw her bring beer in for the boys, and I heard the way they were talking and carrying on."

"Sasha knows that Jacob is at an age where boys tend to go wild, so she thinks if she keeps the party at our house she'll be able to manage him better and he won't be going off and getting into trouble."

"Damn, Josh, she is the trouble. Why can't you open your eyes? Soon it's going to be too late. If you don't come home and put a stop to this, I'm calling Children's Services."

"Now I see this for what it is. You want my kids. Well, Momma, you're not going to get them. Sasha is a wonderful woman, and a great step-mother. She and I will make decisions about our children, and you can stay out of it, or forget that I'm your son."

That ended the conversation. I didn't send the girls home that night. The next day I drove them to school and told them I would pick them up. When the afternoon rolled around and I went to get them a security guard met me at my car and ordered me off the school property. Josh had told the principal I was no longer allowed to pick up the girls.

I had to sit back and watch as Sasha drove away with them. My stomach churned and I felt sick wondering what sort of punishment she'd subject those sweet, innocent girls to. All that I could do for the time being was to worry. Then I thought of a way that I might be able to force Sasha's hand. Gwen Taylor lived next door to Josh. She'd known him before Benita died. I called her.

"I'm worried about my grandchildren," I said.

"You should be, with the ruckus going on over there all the time, and the cars coming and leaving," Gwen said.

"I've tried to do something about it, but Josh won't let me," I said.

"Rita, for the life of me I don't know why your son married that woman. She's nothing but a two-bit whore that used to work in a bar out by the factory. I heard all about her from my nephew who works with Josh. A woman like her shouldn't be around children. Shoot, I heard that she had two kids of her own that she left with her sister so she could take the job stripping."

"Josh told me that Sasha was a maid at a motel before they got married."

"That woman might have worked on beds, but it wasn't making them up. Call my nephew. I'll give you his number. He'll fill you in on Miss Sasha."

I made the call. Gwen's nephew, Paul was happy to fill me in on

Sasha's past. He also said he tried to talk Josh out of marrying her, but Josh was so taken by her looks that he couldn't think straight. My son thought marriage would change Sasha. Instead it had been a springboard for her to set herself up in a better life.

"I'm not surprised at what she's doing," Paul said. "Those boys are probably spending their whole allowance for a chance to have sex with a woman like her. When Sasha worked at the Whistling Pig she didn't do anything unless she got paid."

"Did Josh know?"

"He had to, but it didn't matter. Josh went nuts over Sasha. The girls aren't supposed to date the customers, but after she found out that he had a good job and owned his own home, Sasha didn't care. She set her sights on Josh and she got him."

I couldn't imagine my decent son sitting in a sleazy strip bar flirting with a woman like Sasha, much less marrying her and trusting her with his children. Knowing what I now knew, I was convinced more than ever that I had to get my grandchildren out of that house. I couldn't think about Josh's feelings when their safety was at stake.

My next phone call was to Child Services. I was asked dozens of questions, and in the end they told me that unless there was some evidence of wrong doing their hands were tied. By this time I was frantic. Everywhere I turned I hit a brick wall.

Arthur basically told me to leave things alone and they'd work themselves out, but all I could think of was what might happen to Tamara and Angel if Sasha carried through on her threat.

After another month, and the end of the school term coming to a close, I knew I had to take action. At least when the girls were in school they were safe. I called Gwen and asked her if she would help me with a plan to put an end to the wild goings on. It took a lot of persuading, but she finally agreed.

That night I went to her house. We listened as the music grew louder, and watched more young men coming into the house. I'd seen the girls enter earlier, driven home by Jacob, but Sasha wasn't around. And unless we could catch Sasha in on the party, there were lots of ways she could wiggle out of trouble.

When she did come home, she had cases of beer in her car. Jacob and another boy helped her bring them into the house. Gwen and I waited an hour before she called the police, reporting a disturbance next door. She also mentioned that she thought there were underage boys and girls in the house.

Together we listened for the sirens. As they came closer, my hopes grew that someone would now do something to save my grandchildren. Three police cars parked at the curb, and officers converged on the house. Kids began scrambling out the back door, and some crawled out windows trying to get away, but they were rounded up and hand-cuffed. I watched Sasha, who was practically naked, being hauled to a police car, and then saw Angel and Tamara come out.

Gwen and I went to the officer who seemed to be in charge and told him what we knew. I asked if I could take Angel and Tamara with me, but he refused. They would have to be processed and put in a foster home first, and then I could petition for custody of them. I gave the officer the number where he could reach my son.

I thought that my problems were over, but they'd only just begun. Sasha was charged with contributing to the delinquency of minors, and the boys, including Jacob, were put into Juvenile Detention. Angel and Tamara were turned over to social workers and placed in a foster home.

Josh was furious. . .but not with Sasha. He blamed me. And he also bailed Sasha out of jail. My actions, done to rescue my grandchildren, had only served to punish them and allow the guilty party to go free. Gwen told me that Sasha was back to her old ways the minute Josh left town, only now it was men who came over and usually during the day.

There was only one way to convince my son that I was telling the truth, and that was for him to see Sasha in the act with another man. Driven by desperation, I placed a call to him and told him that his father had suffered a heart attack. Then I prayed that God wouldn't punish me for lying by making my lie come true. I asked Josh to come straight to the hospital, and not to worry about calling Sasha; I'd get in touch with her.

I waited at the entrance to the hospital until I saw Josh. Hoping to stop him before he learned I'd lied; I ran to his truck and told him, "Sasha's car is broken down so she wants us to pick her up at home. Daddy is stable for now, so let's hurry to your house to get Sasha."

Gwen was watching for me, and she called my cellular to let me know when a man was at the house. On the drive there, Josh asked questions about Arthur, and I fielded them the best that I could. We pulled into his driveway.

"Whose car is that?" he asked, referring to the Mercedes parked behind Sasha's car.

"I don't know," I said. "Let's go on in and get Sasha. I want to get back to the hospital."

Josh and I walked at a quick pace up the steps. He unlocked the door and we went inside. The house seemed empty, except for some romantic music playing on the CD player.

"She must be here," Josh said. "Her car's out front, and she'd never leave the CD player on."

"Maybe she's upstairs," I said.

Josh walked ahead of me on the stairs. We reached the landing and heard the unmistakable sounds of love making coming from the master bedroom at the end of the hallway.

I gazed into my son's dark eyes and saw his confusion. He brushed past me and raced to the bedroom, where he flung open the door. I could see Sasha on the bed, completely naked, with a man, who was also naked. Modesty prevents my saying what they were doing.

"Sasha, how could you?" Josh screamed. I could hear his heart breaking and hated myself for what I'd done to him.

She shot up off the bed and began giving Josh some lame excuse. The man hurried to put his clothes on. Josh started for him, but I moved faster and stepped between them. "Get out of here now if you know what's good for you," I said. The man didn't have to be told twice.

Josh was a ball of fury. I could tell that he wanted to tear Sasha to pieces. "Think of the children, Josh," I said. "She's not worth going to prison over. You have three precious children who need their father. Throw this woman out on her sorry butt and do something to get your kids back."

It was the first time in months that he actually listened to me and took my advice. "Sasha," Josh said, "I want you out of here now. Take your clothes, and your car, and never set foot in this house again. If you give me any trouble I'll have you charged with rape of a minor. Momma told me about you and Jacob. I didn't believe her because I didn't want to believe her, but now I know she was right."

Sasha began throwing clothes from the closet onto the bed. The look she gave me could have cut open a boulder in one slice. Josh and I waited down stairs until Sasha left. He cried, thinking about what a fool he'd been and the mess he'd made of his children's lives.

"You need to dry up those tears and start thinking about what you can do to help your children," I said. "Josh, they needed you, and they still do."

The next day my son began the journey to reclaiming his children. It wasn't easy, because he had to convince the authorities that it was in the best interest of the children that they live with him. If Sasha was in the picture at all, Josh couldn't get his kids back.

A temporary measure was to place them with Arthur and me. We gladly took them in. Six months later, the children were returned to their father. Josh admitted that he'd been wrong to rush into marriage with Sasha, and that he hadn't gotten to know her well because he was too consumed by her sexy looks.

It's been a year since Sasha went out of our lives, and in that time Josh has gone on some dates with decent women, but he assures me he's not in a hurry to marry anyone soon. His main objective is being the best father he can be, and for that, I'm proud to call him my son.

THE END

TEENAGE VIXEN
She Made Our Father Cancel
Our Wedding Plans

I couldn't believe my eyes. Marlon had told me that he had a thirteen-year-old daughter, but the girl with him looked at least eighteen. She was tall, and well developed, and as soon as Marlon and I got married she'd be my step-daughter. I wanted her to like me, but all I could see in her dark brown eyes was trouble.

Still, I did my best. "Samantha, your father tells me you're going to attend Ralston Jr. High," I said.

"I guess so," she said in a moody voice. "I wish I could still go to my other school, but the School Board said I have to go in the district where I live and Daddy won't move."

Marlon looked as uncomfortable as I felt. Samantha had moved in with him after he and I became engaged. She wasn't getting along with her mother, and from everything Marlon said, the problem had to do with his ex-wife's boyfriends.

"Cheryl teaches at the high school," Marlon told Samantha, making an attempt to find some common ground. "She'll be right across the street from your school. Maybe the two of you can have lunch together?" Samantha shrugged indifferently.

"How do you like living at your Dad's?" I asked.

"Daddy's apartment is a lot smaller than Momma's house. He barely has room for two people."

"Then I'd say it's lucky we're going to live in my house. I have three bedrooms, and we can ride to school together. And my house has a large den that we can turn into a game room. You can entertain your friends there."

Samantha glanced at Marlon, and then back at me. "I don't have any friends here, so I won't need a room to entertain them. Besides, I'd rather just live with Daddy than move into a stranger's house."

Marlon looked miserable, but what had he expected? To Samantha I was the 'other woman' who was taking her mother's place. To me she was the threat to my happiness and the life I'd imagined with Marlon.

Of course I knew he had a daughter from his previous marriage. He'd told me up front about his marriage and how it had fallen apart when his wife began an affair with a friend of his.

Marlon and I had met at the school where I worked. He was a foreman on the city's grounds keeping crew, and was in charge of maintaining the football field. The teachers' parking lot was close to where the crew kept its heavy equipment. One day I came out to find I had a flat tire. Marlon stepped up to change it for me, and to reward him, the next day I brought him some cookies I'd baked.

Soon we were having lunch together, followed by dinners and casual dates. After a couple of months our dates became less casual. We were falling in love. Marlon, who was six years older than I was, had married young. He'd gotten his girlfriend pregnant and being a decent man, had done the right thing and married her. While Marlon worked, Louise, his wife, stayed at home with Samantha. When Samantha was nine, Louise began an affair, which ended the marriage.

Though I was sorry that Marlon had gone through such a rough time, I was happy that I'd found my soul mate, and I wasn't going to let him go. Somehow, I had to get through to Samantha.

"Samantha, you know your father and I are getting married. When we do, my house will be our house. Yours as well as mine."

She slowly lowered, and then raised her thick eyelashes. There was a nasty smile on her full lips. "That's a long way off."

"No it isn't," I said. "It's next month."

Marlon looked sheepish. What had he done? There was something he hadn't told me. Before he could get a word out, Samantha let me know about the new plans. "Daddy said he was going to put it off until I got adjusted," she said.

"Really? He hasn't said a word about postponing it to me."

"Maybe he doesn't tell you everything."

I glared at Marlon. "Is it true, Marlon? You want to postpone our wedding?"

"I was going to talk to you about it tonight. Samantha needs some time to adjust to living with me and I thought things would go smoother for everyone if we gave her time to get to know you before you and I jumped into marriage."

"Jumped into marriage? We've had this wedding planned for months." I'd never been so angry in my life. How dare he back out of the wedding after all the plans we'd made and the money I'd spent. "Guess I'll go on home now. I have a hundred people to contact; people that expect to be at our wedding next month. And there are all the other arrangements that I'll have to call off. I hope I can get some of my deposits back." I picked up my purse and jacket, and then stormed out of the pizza parlor.

Marlon followed behind me. "Wait, Cheryl, don't be like this."

I whirled around and faced him. "Marlon, you're making a huge mistake. Samantha will never be adjusted enough to see you married to anyone other than her mother. Kids are like that. And if you let her push you into calling off our wedding, she'll get the idea she's in charge. God help you if that happens."

"I'm not calling off the wedding--just putting it on hold for a while."

"Baby, she's just a kid. I'm her daddy, and I have to think of her needs."

"We could both think of her needs if you would stand with me on this. Please don't postpone the wedding. Marlon, it will break my heart. My parents are flying up from Florida. Your mother is coming from Baltimore. There has to be some sort of compromise."

"I don't want to put the wedding off any more than you do, but Samantha can't handle me getting married right now."

"Bull. What she really wants is to break us up, and so far her scheme is working."

Samantha came out of the pizza parlor. "Daddy, they want their money. You'd better pay them before they call the cops to you."

"Cheryl, I've got to go. I'll call you later." Marlon left me standing on the sidewalk and hurried to Samantha. I watched as they went into the pizza parlor arm in arm.

I'd never been so crushed. Marlon Gaffney was my heart. And yes, I'll admit my pride was wounded, too. Having to face my family and friends with the news that Marlon wanted to put the wedding on hold was painfully embarrassing.

When Marlon called later that night we were just into our conversation when Samantha picked up the phone. "Daddy, how much longer you gonna be?" she asked. "I promised to call Momma and let her know how I'm doing."

"I'll be right off," he said. I couldn't believe it. "Cheryl, we'll talk tomorrow. Samantha needs the phone."

"So I heard. Marlon, couldn't she have called her mother before you got on the phone? Or at least had the good manners to wait until you and I finished our conversation?"

"Please don't start up again. I'm worn out. I'll talk to you tomorrow."

He hung up. Usually when our conversations ended we would tell each other "I love you." But Marlon had simply hung up on me without even saying "good-night." We had a problem that was only going to get worse if Samantha had her way.

That night I went to bed and cried myself to sleep. When I woke the next morning sunlight was pouring through my windows and birds were singing. It didn't matter though. There could have been a storm and gray clouds for all I cared. At least the storm would match my mood.

I dressed, gathered my things, and left for work. As I was going into the high school I saw Marlon and Samantha going into the junior high. She was in eighth grade. I was grateful that I wouldn't have her in my classes.

When school was dismissed for the day I headed for my car. There was a group of kids gathered beside the school bus pick-up. Most of them were boys, and at the center of the group was Samantha. She certainly hadn't wasted any time making friends. I considered offering her a ride home, but then changed my mind. If I did anything to embarrass her in front of the other kids it would be one more problem between us.

All that week I noticed the circle of boys around Samantha was growing; however, the girls wanted nothing to do with her. I thought Marlon should know what was going on, so when we went out that Friday night I told him.

"It worries me that she might be sending out all the wrong signals," I said. "You know how teenage boys are. Worse yet, some of those boys hanging around her are rumored to be in gangs, and they're not junior high boys. A couple of them are in my social studies class and they have a lot of attitude."

"Oh, Cheryl, you're making too much of this," Marlon said. "Samantha spends most of her time with a girl who lives in the apartment complex next to ours. Her name is Latoya. Matter of fact, Samantha is spending the night there tonight. Latoya is helping her catch up on math."

"Have you met Latoya and her family?"

"Not yet, but Samantha says they're nice folks. Cheryl, I try not to press her too hard about her friends. I don't want her to think I don't trust her."

He was making a huge mistake, but I didn't say anything else. This was my time with Marlon and I had my own agenda to attend to. "Marlon, I haven't sent out notices that the wedding has been cancelled yet. I was hoping you would reconsider."

He looked down at his plate of food as he raked his fork through his baked potato. "Cheryl, honey, I can't rush Samantha. When we set the date for the wedding I had no idea that my teenage daughter would end up living with me. It all happened so suddenly. Now I have an obligation to put her needs first. We're adults, Cheryl. We can afford to be generous and give Samantha the time she needs."

I felt like tossing my plate of lasagna in his face. Instead I mentally counted to ten, took a deep breath, let it out, and said, "That would be fine, except I've spent a lot of money on this wedding. Most of my savings have gone into it. I'll lose my deposits, and I won't have the money to put into another wedding later."

"Then we'll just go to the court house and get married," he said. "We don't need a big wedding as long as we have each other."

Tears welled in my eyes. I wanted a real wedding, with flowers and bridesmaids. Marlon didn't make as much money as I did, so I'd taken on all of the expenses except the honeymoon, which was going to be a weekend getaway in the mountains because that was all he could afford.

"Doesn't anything I want matter to you? Will the rest of my life be spent bowing down to Samantha?"

Marlon clinched his jaws, and his eyes narrowed. "Cheryl, don't make me choose between you and my only child. That would be a huge mistake on your part, because as a father, my daughter has to come first."

"Did she come first when you were married to Louise? You told me that when you were married to Louise you always put her first. Now I am relegated to second place in your life. It isn't fair to me."

"You're being childish," he said. "I think we should call an end to this evening before one of us says something they can't take back."

We needed to talk, and to work through our problems. Marlon was right, though. The more we said the more we risked destroying our future together. This was our first fight and I didn't know how to handle it.

The drive home was silent except for the sound of the radio. He let me out in front of my house. I paused, wanting to hear him say he loved me, but he was too angry. It was a side of Marlon I hadn't seen, and after seeing it, I didn't like it one bit.

Over the weekend I sat by the phone waiting for his call that never came. Late Sunday night I began writing notes to all the guests we'd invited to the wedding, telling them that it had been postponed indefinitely.

The next day at school I went to the teacher's lounge for some coffee. I was surprised to see Hazel Jackson there. She taught at the junior high. "Hazel, surely our coffee isn't that much better than the coffee in your lounge," I said.

"I'm not here for the coffee, Cheryl," she said. "We need to talk about Marlon Gaffney's daughter. She's way out of control. This morning I caught her with one of the high school boys in the band room. He was all over her. If I hadn't walked in on them when I did, I don't have a doubt in my head they would have had sex right there."

"Hazel, she's only thirteen years old. I know she looks older, but she's just a kid."

"Kids like her are having kids of their own all the time. Marlon needs to be told, and I thought it would be better if you talked to him. I have to get back to class."

"I'll walk you over," I said. Hazel and I walked through the high school. As we passed some of my students they greeted me with "Hey, Miss Baxter" and "What's up, Miss B." I enjoyed the fact that I was a popular teacher; and it proved I could get along with kids.

At the junior high I went with Hazel to her lounge, where I was able to talk to a few other teachers that had Samantha in their classes. They all said the same thing. Samantha paid no attention to her studies. She was fixated on boys. None of the girls liked her, but the boys thought she was hot.

"She has one friend named Latoya that she studies with," I said. "Is Latoya in her classes?"

"What's Latoya's last name?" Hazel asked. "Cheryl, we have dozens of girls by that name in this school."

"Marlon didn't say," I said. "Please, if anything happens that he should know about, come to me and I'll talk to him."

They all agreed to keep watch over Samantha and to let me know if something happened. I went back to my class, but all I could think about was Samantha and wondered how I would tell her father about her conduct.

As soon as I got home I called Marlon at work. His voice was light and cheerful. "Baby, I'm glad you called. I was afraid you were still mad at me because of the wedding. Glad to see you've come to your senses."

I almost hung up on him. "Marlon, I'm not calling about the wedding. I've permanently postponed it, and I've started sending back the wedding presents. What I'm calling about is your daughter. Her conduct is getting out of hand."

He groaned. "You just won't give up, will you? From the second you laid eyes on Samantha you have resented her. So what is it now?"

"She's making out with high school boys, and she's not paying attention in class because all she thinks about is boys."

"That's a damn lie," he bellowed. "I know my baby, and she'd never do anything like that. She's still a little girl. If boys notice her, it's not her fault. She can't help it if she looks older than she is."

"They are doing more than noticing her. Marlon, I only called to tell you that you have a problem that could get much worse if you don't do something about it now. At least talk to her mother. Maybe letting her move in with you wasn't such a good idea."

He was quiet for a few seconds, and then gave a low chuckle. "I get it. You want me to send her home so we can go back to how we were before she moved in. It's not going to happen, Cheryl."

Marlon hung up on me. Then and there I made up my mind that I'd stay out of his business. If his daughter became the school tramp, then it was up to him to handle her. He'd let me know where I stood, and as much as I hated losing this man that I loved so much, I wasn't going to let him walk all over me.

As the days passed more rumors about Samantha surfaced. I did my best to ignore them. Marlon and I hardly talked anymore, and when we did it was awkward. He'd taken a part time night job at a factory that made boxes. Even though he no longer paid child support, Samantha had proven to be quite expensive. Marlon couldn't say no to her and gave her everything she asked for.

One evening Hazel and I went to dinner and a movie. When we came out we saw a group of kids loitering around the parking-lot at the multiplex. Samantha was in the group, and wearing Anton Smith's bright red jacket. She held a beer in one hand and a cigarette in the other.

"Cheryl, we have to do something," Hazel said. "Samantha shouldn't be with that crowd. At least call Marlon and tell him where she is."

"Marlon and I are hardly speaking and she's the reason, Hazel. He doesn't believe anything I tell him about Samantha. She has him convinced I'm out to get her."

"Well we can't ignore this. Anton has a reputation for being rough with girls. We have to do something."

Hazel was right. Anton Smith was in one of my classes, though he seldom bothered to come to class. Samantha was in over her head. No matter how much she hated me, she was still a child and I couldn't leave her with those wolves.

"Let's go talk to them." Hazel and I walked up to the group. They stopped talking when they saw us. I spoke first, "Samantha, I'll bet your daddy doesn't know you're with these kids."

She gave me a snide look. "What's it to you, Miss Baxter? What I do, or what my daddy does is none of your business. He dumped you, remember."

"I remember, but when I find you hanging out and drinking with these boys I make it my business. Samantha, either you come with us now or I will make a call to the juvenile authorities." I heard a couple of boys snicker and turned to face off with them. "You won't think it's so funny when they haul you in for contributing to the delinquency of a minor. She's only thirteen years old."

"She's old enough for me," Anton said. "With a body like that, it don't matter how old she is. Way I see it, she's a woman."

"Unfortunately for you, the law sees it different, and if you're having sex with her you're committing statutory rape," Hazel said. "Anton, go home now. Samantha, is leaving with us."

Anton stepped toward Hazel and gave her a shove. She tumbled to the ground, hitting it hard. I stooped beside her to help her up. The group seemed stunned by what Anton had done, but once he began to chuckle, they all laughed.

"Y'all get on home," he told us. "We don't need no old ladies hassling us. If you mess with me or Samantha you're going to be sorry."

His threats weren't to be taken lightly. I'd heard stories about how he'd beaten his own mother. Anton respected no one. "Come on, Hazel," I said. "We have other ways of handling this."

Hazel and I went to my car. Once we were a block away from the multiplex I took out my cellular and dialed 911 to report what had happened. Despite Anton's threats, I had to at least try to get Samantha away from him and his gang.

We waited until the police arrived and arrested the lot of them for underage drinking and loitering. Afterward we drove to the police station to file a complaint against Anton. Samantha had given them a fake name and address, as well as telling the officers that she was eighteen. They seemed to believe her until Hazel and I told them the truth.

Marlon was called at work and told to come to the station. I hoped that at last he would see the trouble his daughter was in and do something to put a stop to it. Instead of putting a stop to her wild ways, Marlon took Samantha's side. After talking to her, he decided that the whole thing was my fault. Hazel and I were two old busy bodies, and the kids were just hanging out listening to music.

"They did a breathalyzer test on her, Marlon," I said. "She was drinking and the police can prove it. God only knows what else she's been doing. I tried to warn you, but you wouldn't listen to me."

"When it comes down to believing my own flesh and blood, or believing a woman who has it in for her, I'm going to believe my daughter every time," he said. "Samantha couldn't help it if the girls she went to the movies with left her to go after some boys. She was just trying to get a ride home."

"We offered her a ride home, Marlon. Hazel and I both wanted to get her away from those boys. Samantha wouldn't leave with us. And her boyfriend even knocked Hazel down. Is Anton Smith the kind of boy you want your daughter dating?"

"I don't know Anton Smith, but I know you." He stormed away from me and went to talk to an officer. I grabbed Hazel and headed for my car. I promised myself to never again interfere. I was done with Marlon and Samantha.

My promise to myself was short lived, though. On the day that would have been my wedding day, I lounged around the house, watched a DVD, and did everything except think about Marlon. It was close to eleven when he called.

"Cheryl, I need your help. I know I don't have any right to ask for it, but I need you. Samantha has cleaned out everything in my apartment and has run off with Anton."

"Call the police. She's underage. I'm sure they'll do something to help you find her."

"If I call them Samantha will end up in juvenile. The court will take her away from me. Please, help me find her. You know Anton Smith and the people he hangs around with. I don't think they've left the state. A neighbor saw the kids loading things into a van and asked Samantha what was going on. Samantha told him she was moving back to her mother's house. I talked to Louise and she said Samantha hasn't called her in a couple of weeks."

"Do you believe Louise?"

"Yeah, I believe her. Cheryl, there's something you don't know. The reason Louise asked me to take Samantha was because she caught Samantha in bed with an older man. Louise thought Samantha needed a firmer hand and that I would keep her in line."

I was stunned. Marlon had been given fair warning about his daughter's wild side, and he'd done nothing to stop her. "Why didn't you do something when you had a chance, Marlon? Now could be too late."

He was silent for a second, and when he spoke again, I could tell he was choking back sobs. "Samantha said it was Louise who had a problem. She said Louise was jealous of her because the men Louise dated were paying more attention to her than to her mother. I wanted to believe Samantha, so I did."

I agreed to help him. While I waited for Marlon to pick me up I made a list of people I'd seen Samantha with. I also suspected that the electronics had been sold and told Marlon as much.

"To hell with my things, I want to find Samantha."

We drove to Anton's house. His mother said she hadn't seen him in days, but suspected he was hanging out with Leroy Thomas. My heart sank. Leroy was bad news. He'd dropped out of school two years ago, and everyone said he was selling drugs and running prostitutes.

"Marlon, we should call the police. Leroy is rough, and I'm sure he has guns."

"I can't call the police. I'll lose Samantha if I do. A social worker came to see me and said I had to get a better handle on Samantha or the state would take custody of her."

"Maybe that would have been best. You've been blind to Samantha since she moved in with you. Marlon, she's in trouble. I wouldn't doubt it if Leroy and Anton are prostituting her to get money for drugs."

"Damn, Cheryl, what have I done? I wanted to be a good father, and I sacrificed everything that I cared about to make Samantha happy. Now she could be in real danger."

There were tears in his eyes, and he looked like he'd aged ten years in the past six weeks. How much hell had his teenage vixen put him through? Mrs. Smith had given us Leroy's address. Marlon and I drove

106

to the west side of town, down a street of deteriorating houses, cars on blocks, and scattered trash on porches.

We spotted the address and slowed to take a look. The house was close to falling in on itself, and in the driveway there were half a dozen cars parked at odd angles. He pulled to the curb and turned off the engine. "What are you going to do?" I asked. "Go up to the door, knock and ask if she's there? Marlon, please call the police."

"Wait in the car. If I'm not out in five minutes, you can call the cops. I'm going to drag Samantha out of there by her hair if I have to."

"She might not even be there. And they could have guns."

Marlon ignored my fears and bounded from the car. He ran up the rickety steps to the door. I rolled down the window so I could hear what was going on. Blaring music made it difficult, but I was able to make out what he was saying.

"Send Samantha Gaffney out right now," he yelled.

"Hey, old man, wait your turn. Samantha can't do everybody at once."

Marlon grabbed the younger man and threw him off the porch. Soon a group of people came out of the house. I saw Anton, and in his hand was a gun. Damn Marlon's pride; I called the police.

Leroy and Marlon continued to fight. Samantha came running out of the house half dressed. Someone grabbed her and held her back. Marlon heard her scream and tried to get to her. The pop of a gunshot went off and Marlon fell to the ground.

In the distance came the sound of police sirens. As the sound drew nearer people scattered. Most got into cars; causing a traffic jam in the driveway as they tried to escape. I knelt beside Marlon, weeping and begging him not to die. Blood was everywhere. The man who'd held Samantha back released her. She ran to her father, screaming and hysterical.

I wanted to shout at her; to slap her arrogant face. She was the reason Marlon had been shot. If he died, his blood was on her hands. But yelling at Samantha wasn't going to save Marlon's life. I took off my sweater and held it against his wound in hopes of stopping the flow of blood. He moaned softly and slipped into unconsciousness.

Hands pulled me from Marlon. It was the paramedics. They began working on Marlon. I prayed for God to save him. A gurney was brought out and Marlon was placed upon it. "We're taking him to Jefferson Memorial Hospital," the lead paramedic said. "You can follow us there if you have a car, or the police will give you a ride."

Samantha stood shivering and sobbing. Marlon's jacket was in the car. I got it and gave it to her. "Come on, we should be with him," I said. "And the police will want to talk to both of us."

The longest night of my life began. Marlon was rushed to surgery, and all I could do was wait. Louise came to the hospital, and to my surprise, I liked her. Samantha had calmed down, and when the police tried to talk to her the old arrogance came back. She refused to say anything about Anton or Leroy.

Louise asked for a few moments alone with Samantha. After their talk, Samantha's attitude had completely changed and she admitted everything. She and Anton had stolen from Marlon so they could get enough money to go in with Leroy on a drug buy. Samantha had prostituted herself to come up with the rest of the cash they needed.

I had seen Anton shoot Marlon. Samantha validated my statement. Arrest warrants were put out for Leroy and Anton. As for Samantha, Louise was going to take custody of her again if the social worker would permit it. Samantha would be sent to a school for troubled girls where she could get the help she needed.

Marlon survived, but was in critical condition for days. Eventually he healed enough to go home. He still needed care, though, so I arranged for him to move into my house. We hired a nurse to be with him during the day, and I took care of him at night until he was well.

Maybe some day we will find our way back to being lovers, but that will require an effort because I am not able to live with a person who doesn't trust my word. I often think how different all our lives would have been if only Marlon hadn't put his faith in an over-sexed child instead of being the kind of father a girl like Samantha needed.

THE END

LIES & DECEIT
I Believed Everything He Said!

There was so much love and pride in my heart that I almost burst wide open as I listened to Josh preach his first sermon. This was our dream coming true. After so many years of trying to find a paying job in a church, Josh had finally landed one. He wasn't the pastor yet, but he was the assistant, as well as music director.

His clear, bold voice filled the room. The congregation shouted, "Amen," after practically everything Josh said. After church everyone shook Josh's hand, and told him what a powerful sermon he'd delivered. Pastor Andrew took me aside and said, "Lena, your husband is a real blessing to this congregation."

"Thank you, Pastor Andrew," I said. "I feel the same way; blessed that he's my husband."

Driving home afterwards, Josh sang all the way there. He'd never been so happy, and neither had I. He was proving my parents wrong. They hadn't wanted me to marry him. Daddy thought he was lazy, and Momma thought there was something shifty about him, but I knew Josh, and I had faith in him and his dreams.

I made a quick lunch for us, and then changed my clothes to go to work at the hospital, where I worked cleaning the floors and rooms. I had two jobs: one at the hospital, and another part time job at a motel as a maid. We needed the money. Though Josh was being paid, it wasn't enough to make ends meet and pay off old debts.

"Baby, I wish you could stay a little longer," he said. "We could cuddle up in bed and really celebrate."

"I'll be home before you know it, so hold the thought." Besides being a great preacher and singer, my husband could make love like nobody else. All the time I was working my thoughts would drift back to my husband. I'd always known he was something special, and now others were seeing it, too. When my shift ended and I drove home, ready for our special celebration. Josh fixed a bubble bath for us.

As we soaked and talked, his hands found my breasts and began massaging them with oil. Just his touch could get me so hot that nothing else was required, but that wasn't Josh's way. He made love slowly, and wouldn't hurry no matter how much I begged him. We moved together, surrounding each other's body with our legs, and touching each other all over.

Our moans of pleasure filled the room, and when the time was right, we stepped from the tub and made love on the floor. Josh was a man who could go all night long, and make me want more of him. We helped each other dry off and moved to our bed, where the celebration continued for hours.

A few months later Pastor Andrew and the congregation asked Josh to take on more duties. The church had toyed with the idea of a teen ministry, and Pastor Andrew thought Josh was the man to head it. Members of the congregation worked to transform the old chapel into a special church just for our teenagers. Josh preached there every Sunday. He received a small salary increase as well.

"Honey, the way things are going I'll be able to quit one of my jobs soon and we can get busy making a baby," I said.

"Not so fast, Lena," Josh said. "We're still a long way from paying off our debts. The baby making will have to wait at least another year."

"That's a year sooner than it was last year," I said, feeling that the road ahead was going to be a good one for us.

Josh worked hard with the teens. He had after school programs that kept them busy and away from the drug scene and gangs. His new ministry was having an affect on Josh. He dressed younger, picked up some hip-hop phrases he'd never used, and even had his hair styled to fit in with his congregation.

At first it amused me and I teased him about the changes. Then the bills started coming in. He had charge accounts in stores all over town, and instead of our debt going down, it was going up.

"Josh, you've got to stop spending. Just last month you charged more than you made. I can't afford to pay the utilities if I have to cover all these new bills." My tone was a lot harsher than I wanted it to be.

"Lena, I have to fit in with the kids if I'm going to have any influence on them. We've had dozens join the church since I took over as teen pastor. Most of those kids used to sleep when Pastor Andrew preached. They couldn't identify with him."

"Hon, you're doing a wonderful job, and it's important, but we don't have extra money for you to spend like you've been spending. Do you think you might be able to pick up a part time job somewhere?"

"I'm doing the Lord's work, Lena. It's a full time job. Cut back on some of the household expenses if you have to."

I wondered what he wanted me to cut down on. Household expenses were already down to the bone. We couldn't cut them anymore and still have electricity, water, food, and a roof over our heads.

Each Sunday I attended the adult church. I'd wanted to go to the teen services to hear Josh, but he insisted that I stay away. "Having grownups there intimidates the kids," he told me.

The kids, especially the girls, treated him like he was a rock star. They surrounded him when church services ended, each one trying to get his attention. Often they called him at home to discuss their problems. We never had an uninterrupted hour together, unless we were sleeping. Even our sex life suffered. More often than not, even if we were in the act of making love, the phone would ring and Josh would answer it.

On my night off I was often alone because he had choir practice or counseling sessions. When our anniversary rolled around I was determined to have my husband to myself for one night.

He wasn't home when I got there, so I called the church. The secretary told me Josh was out. He'd gone to the high school talent show to see some of the kids compete. It was an afternoon event and should be over no later than five.

Five passed, and I hadn't heard from Josh. Soon it was six, then seven, and before I knew it, midnight was approaching. For the first time in our marriage he'd forgotten our anniversary.

When he came home it was nearly one in the morning. He undressed and flopped into bed. "Where have you been?" I demanded.

"Lena, I'm tired," he said. "Let's talk in the morning."

"No. I've been waiting for you all night, and I'd like an explanation. Josh, don't you remember what today is?"

He was quiet for a few minutes, and then let out a groan. "Oh, baby, I'm so sorry. I absolutely lost track of the date. Don't be mad, Lena, I'll make it up to you. We'll go out to dinner this weekend." He stroked my hair and put his arm around me.

"I can't. I took tonight off, and that means I'll have to work all weekend."

"Okay, we'll do it the weekend after."

"You still haven't told me where you were."

I felt him stiffen. "Woman, I'm the head of this house. I don't answer to you. You answer to me." He was yelling so loudly that the neighbors banged on the wall.

"What is wrong with you?" I asked, trying to get him to calm down. "I've never heard you talk this way before. And I don't like it one bit. You stood me up on our anniversary, and I'm not even allowed to ask you where you were?"

"Fine, I'll tell you where I was. Some of the kids from the church were in a talent show at school. They won, and I took them out for pizza to celebrate. Afterwards, I went back to the church for a counseling session with the parents of a boy who got shot because he wanted to get out of a gang."

I'd never felt so selfish. "Why didn't you tell me that when you came in?"

"Because I didn't want to talk about it. Lena, I was the one who talked him into leaving the gang. I feel responsible."

"It's not your fault," I said, and took Josh in my arms. My lips covered his, and I kissed him as tenderly as possible, trying to give him the comfort I knew he needed. He pulled me closer and ran his hand down my back and lower. I could feel him getting hard with desire.

In seconds we were making love, only it wasn't slow and easy. Josh became rough and demanding. At first I was a little excited; then grew frightened. It seemed as though he wanted to hurt me. He held my arms in a tight grip against the bed, and his kisses bruised my lips.

When he reached orgasm he rolled off me and went to sleep. Something was wrong in my marriage and it wasn't all about a kid getting shot. I've never been the kind of person who confronts problems head on. Sometimes I ignore them in hopes they'll resolve themselves. I never brought up the subject of our anniversary night again.

Soon I wasn't able to attend church at all. I had to work. Instead of a full time and a part time job, I now had two full time jobs. Josh and I were seldom home at the same time. He spent lots of time taking the youth choir to competitions around the state.

Josh spent the money I earned long before I got my payday. He charged meals at restaurants, charged hotel rooms for the kids and him, and was constantly buying new clothes. If I complained he became indignant. We argued about money all the time.

A year had passed since Josh preached his first sermon at the church. Any time I had off from work was spent washing clothes, keeping up the house, and sleeping so I could start it all again the next day. To save money we didn't use the air conditioner unless we were home. One day after work I sat out on the porch, waiting for the house to get cool. Mrs. Guthrie, who lived in the other half of the duplex, came out on the porch and sat in her rocker.

"Lena, you look tuckered out," she said.

"I am, Mrs. Guthrie. And it's so hot inside."

"Can I ask a favor of you?" she said. "I'm probably going to make you mad, like I did Josh, but something has to be done about the noise."

"What noise? Nobody is ever home here, and when we are home, we're sleeping."

"Lena, it's the kids and Josh. Nights, when you're working, they come over and they start up loud music. It goes on until midnight. You know my husband isn't well."

There were never any kids at our house; not that I knew of. "Surely you're mistaken," I said. "Maybe Josh just has the TV too loud."

"I'm not mistaken. I see them coming and going. They park their cars in my driveway. Last week my daughter and son-in-law came for dinner and had to park a block away on account of those kids. Lena, see what you can do about it, or as much as I hate to, I'm going to call the police."

Mrs. Guthrie got up and went inside, slamming her screen door behind her. I didn't know what to think. Josh always told me that teen meetings were conducted at the church in the teen's chapel. When he came home that night I asked him about it.

"We had a couple of socials here," he said. "I invited some of the kids from the choir over for pizza and we practiced a few new numbers. It was only a few times, Lena. That witch next door is exaggerating."

I had never heard him made a disrespectful remark about an older person before. "Her husband is quite ill, Josh."

"Then pray for him and I will, too, but I am entitled to have guests into my home whether she likes it or not."

He stormed past me, out the door, heading for his car. I'd made a pot roast for dinner, his favorite dish. Now I would have to eat alone, again. While getting ready for bed I heard some cars pull into the driveway. Through the curtains I could see flashing blue and red lights.

A hard knock came on the door. I grabbed my robe and went to answer it, fearing something horrible had happened to Josh. Six police officers were crammed onto my small porch. Mrs. Guthrie stood at her door, watching what was going on.

One officer stepped forward. "Is this Josh Phillips' residence?" he asked.

"I'm Lena Phillips," I said. "My husband isn't home. What's this all about?"

"Mrs. Phillips, do you know where your husband is?"

"He's at church with the youth choir; sometimes they practice late."

There was a smirk on the officer's face. I heard another policeman clear his throat and Mrs. Guthrie let out a huffing sound. "Is this about the noise?" I asked the officer. He didn't answer. The police all got into their cars and drove away.

I turned to Mrs. Guthrie. "Do you know why the police come here looking for Josh?"

"I can make a guess," she said. "Maybe if you bothered to go to church sometimes you'd be able to make a guess, too."

"What does that mean?"

"Rumors have been circulating for months about your husband and some of the girls in the youth group. That's why Oh, never mind, you wouldn't believe me if I told you."

I glared at Mrs. Guthrie. What an evil old bat she was to be listening to rumors about Josh. She lived next door to us, and she knew what a good man my husband was. "My husband has put his heart and soul into helping the young people."

"He's put more than that into them," she said, and went inside.

Josh and I weren't getting along, but in my heart I knew he'd never touch another woman, much less a young girl. I went to the phone and called Pastor Andrew. "Pastor, this is Lena Phillips," I said. "The police were just here looking for Josh. Mrs. Guthrie hinted that there were rumors about Josh and some of the teenagers."

"Lena, I'm very sorry all of this has happened," said Pastor Andrew. "I tried to talk to Josh, but he wouldn't listen. That's why I had to stop allowing him to use the chapel at night, and put him on probation. Of course he denies any wrongdoing, but there is just too much talk to the contrary."

"Gossip, you mean. Jealous people who can't control their kids are ashamed because Josh has so much influence over the teenagers and has made a difference when the parents couldn't. I thought you, above all people, would understand and defend him."

"I have defended him, Lena. And he's made me sorry that I did. Josh is ripping the church apart, and what he's done with those kids is an abomination. I didn't know it had gone so far as to involve the police, though."

"Pastor, if Josh isn't at the church, where is he? He told me he was going to rehearse with the youth choir this week to get ready for the competition."

"I don't know what you're talking about," Pastor Andrew said. "Our youth choir hasn't participated in competition in years. We can't afford to send them."

My face burned and I felt sick to my stomach. Obviously Josh had lied to me, but that didn't mean he was doing what Mrs. Guthrie hinted he had done. The phone rang and I answered it.

"Lena, honey, you have to come down to the jail and bail me out," Josh said. "I've been arrested. Someone is falsely accusing me of the most horrible things. I knew there were rumors, and I've done my best to counter them, but someone in the church hates me and won't rest until they've destroy me. I need you, baby."

I could hear the suffering in his voice. Josh was on the verge of tears. In my mind I saw the gentle, good man I married. "Josh, what do they say you've done?"

"Tanya Jeffries has accused me of getting her pregnant. Lena, I never touched the girl. I couldn't do something like that. I love you and I'd never betray you. Tanya has had a crush on me since I took over the youth group. She probably got pregnant by a boy at school, and blamed me because she wants to marry me. I've had to handle her carefully because she's so emotional, so I guess she mistook concern for something else."

Did I believe him? Of course I did. Josh would never have sex with

114

a young girl, and Tanya Jeffries couldn't be more than fifteen years old. "Have they set bail yet?" I asked.

"Not yet, but they will soon. If they won't release me on my own signature, then you'll need to get a bondsman. They charge fifteen percent up front."

"Josh, I only have ten dollars on me, and there's less than fifty in our checking account."

"Lena, get the money. You have to get me out so I can defend myself against these charges. Sell your car."

"If I did that I wouldn't be able to go to work. I'll sell yours."

He grew very quiet. After a few minutes he said, "Am I mistaken to believe that you love me? It sure seems I am, because you're not willing to make even one sacrifice for me. I have to have a car if I'm going to beat these charges. I'll need transportation to get to court and to see lawyers. You can take the bus to work."

The bus stop was half a mile from our house. Still, I understood how upset Josh was, so I didn't argue. "I'll sell my car, but it might take some time."

"We don't have time. Get the money, Lena. And don't say anything to anybody."

Who would I say anything to? There wasn't a person in the town who was a close friend. Working sixteen hours a day didn't make for a full social life. I didn't even know anyone to call about selling my car.

Before I could bail Josh out the police came to the house with a search warrant. I was forced to sit out on the porch while they went through our personal belongings, our papers, and even our trash. Boxes and bags were filled to overflowing. They took more than I thought we owned.

After they allowed me back inside, I was faced with the mess they'd left. For hours I had to put things back into drawers, clear away debris from the floors, and cope with the intrusion into my privacy. Because of everything that was going on, I called into work and said I wouldn't be able to come in.

It was the next day before I was able to bail Josh out. I took my car to a second hand lot. They gave me half of what it was worth, but I had no choice, or time. When I went to find a bondsman I learned what Josh's charges were. He'd been arrested for statutory rape, contributing to the delinquency of a minor, and some other charges I couldn't understand. His bail was twenty thousand dollars. It took all of the money I had gotten for the car to pay the bondsman.

As soon as Josh was free on bail, we sat at home and had a long talk. He convinced me that he was not involved with Tanya sexually. "She's terribly disturbed," he said. "Her home life is a mess and she's looking for a way out."

"But the Jeffries seemed like such nice people. At least I thought so from the brief time I was around them."

"You only came to church a dozen or so times, Lena. That wasn't long enough to get to know anyone. I'm most disappointed in Pastor Andrew. I thought he'd be the first to defend me. He has to know what it's like when a female member of the congregation gets a crush on the pastor. And kids tend to lie and exaggerate more than adults. How could they think I did this?"

"Josh, why did you lie to me about the competitions? Pastor Andrew said that the youth choir hasn't competed in years."

"They haven't. I never said they were competing, only that we were going to the competitions. We go to see what other groups are doing so we can get ideas. Next year I planned to enter our youth choir."

He had me so confused I didn't know what to think. Honestly, I hadn't paid close attention when Josh started talking about the kids, so maybe I had misunderstood. But there were records of motel charges. I mentioned them.

"That just proves I'm telling the truth. If we were competing, the church would have footed the bill instead of me having to pay it."

By nightfall I was convinced that Josh was telling the truth. I promised to help him find a lawyer, and swore to make every sacrifice to pay for a decent attorney. When anyone tried to bring up Josh's arrest I defended him with all of my heart. Once, when in the grocery store, I saw Juanita Jeffries, Tanya's mother. I approached her. She stood like a frozen statue of ice.

"Please, Juanita, talk to me," I said. "How can you believe that my husband abused your daughter? Josh is a good man who only wants the best for the kids. This is a big mistake."

"My husband and I have suffered over this almost as much as Tanya has," Juanita said. "Your husband betrayed our trust and destroyed our family."

"From what I understand, your family was messed up before you even met Josh," I said defiantly. "He tried to help your daughter when you couldn't, and now you're ruining his life."

"Help Tanya? Woman, you're crazy. He didn't help Tanya do anything except get pregnant."

"What makes you so sure that your daughter is pregnant by my husband?"

"Get on away from me or I'll call the police and have you locked up for harassing me. Get on out of here, Lena Phillips. And tell that husband of yours to go to hell."

"I'm not harassing you," I said, trying to keep calm, though I wanted to scratch her eyes out. "All I want is an answer. Why are you blaming Josh?"

"Tanya was a virgin before your husband came along. She hadn't even dated much. Then he started filling her head with the idea that she could be a singing star, and she would sneak off to practice with him."

"That only proves my husband took an interest in her future," I said.

"Yeah, well, he took her to motel rooms to practice, but it wasn't singing. Lena, you're a big fool if you can't see the truth. Josh wasn't helping those kids. He was using them. He liked it when they admired him and made a big fuss over him. They followed him like blind sheep. Tanya wasn't the only girl he took a special interest in. More are coming forward every day."

I turned around and ran from the store. If I allowed myself to believe Juanita I would go crazy. Josh couldn't be the person she described. There couldn't be more girls, unless they had conspired against him out of jealousy. I'd heard of movie and rock stars being blamed for sleeping with underage fans, and sports figures being arrested for rape, only to have the accusations dropped or proven false.

Usually the girls wanted money. But we didn't have money. Josh said Tanya wanted to marry him. That had to be the reason she accused him. To go on with my marriage I had to believe my husband.

While Josh prepared for trial I worked to pay the bills. The attorney was charging a huge fee. We'd had to move into a one room apartment close to where I worked because I couldn't afford bus fare and Josh was too depressed to be depended upon to drive me.

All day each day he sat on the sofa watching television. His reputation had been destroyed, and he was looking at prison time. I wanted to help with the case but wasn't allowed to talk to the attorney. Josh said his communication was privileged, and the attorney didn't want me in their meetings. I accepted this, just as I accepted everything else Josh said.

A year passed and the trial date grew near. Tanya had given birth to a baby girl. Josh was forced to take a DNA test. I was glad he was taking the test because it would prove once and for all that he was innocent. A week before the trial, Josh asked me to go to his attorney's office with him.

To my surprise, Josh had accepted a plea bargain. He would plead guilty in order to get a reduced sentence. "No," I wailed and began weeping. "Why did we fight so hard if you're going to do this? Josh, you're innocent. The DNA will prove you're innocent."

His attorney looked down, unable to meet my gaze. Josh turned his head away. "Someone please tell me what's happening," I said.

"They screwed up on the DNA," Josh said. "I'll bet the Jeffries paid someone off."

I worked in a hospital, and I knew how accurate DNA tests were. And I also knew that the Jeffries didn't have the connections or money to pay anyone off. Even if they did, why would they? There was no reason for them to hate Josh, unless he had impregnated their daughter.

Denial had been a safe place for me, but I could no longer hide there. I had to admit the truth. My husband had been seducing young women. "How long were you sleeping around with those girls?" I demanded to know.

"Lena, you're not turning on me, too," he said. "Baby, I'm innocent."

His attorney stood and walked to the door. "I'll give you people some time alone."

Josh began explaining, telling more lies. I'd heard as many as I could stand. I ran from the office and took a bus to the home of Pastor Andrew. If anyone would tell me the truth, he would. Pastor Andrew welcomed me into his home. His wife got me some iced tea, and left me to talk to Pastor Andrew alone.

"Lena, I'm so sorry," he said. "I understand why you stuck by Josh. He's your husband and you love him. But he's guilty of a lot of wrongdoing. At first things were going so well. He was having a good impact on the teenagers. I guess it all just went to his head. That kind of admiration can affect a man's reasoning."

I remembered other ministers who'd fallen because of their popularity. They thought that they had a free pass to do anything; that they were as important as the God they served. "From what I've learned, everything started when Josh began sleeping with some of the older girls," Pastor Andrew said. "No one knew about it. They didn't talk until after Tanya came forward. In public he was always with a group, but on the side he was seeing girls privately. Some said he took them to motels. Others claimed to have slept with him at your home."

"No, not in our home, on our bed," I said, sobbing. "Did they tell you he made love to them on our bed?"

"I didn't ask for details. Lena, six girls have come forward. The police have proof to substantiate their allegations. There are motel charges on the dates the girls claim to have been with Josh. And your neighbor saw girls going in and out of the house. Besides that, Tanya's baby proved to be Josh's. The DNA test left no doubt he is the father."

There wasn't anything else I needed to hear. I went home, packed my few belongings, and left Josh. I bought a bus ticket back to my hometown, where I had family. My parents, sisters, and brothers were glad to see me, and I'm sure it was tempting, but no one ever said "I told you so". They comforted me and helped me find the strength to go on and start a new life.

Going forward with my life was hard to do. I didn't trust my own judgment anymore. Surely, I should have seen what was going on in my marriage. I guess I just didn't want to know. It was easier to avoid facing the truth than it was to confront it. I suppose I didn't want to lose Josh, so I closed my eyes to what was happening. I'd known something was wrong even before our anniversary and I'd looked the other way.

Now I'm divorced. The attorney my father hired for me saw to it that I wouldn't have to pay Josh's bills. Other than the debts he'd accumulated in order to seduce his young victims, there was nothing else to consider. We owned nothing, and had no money.

I'll always believe that it was pride and vanity that destroyed my husband. He let the praise and compliments go to his head, and turned into the very thing he preached against. Still, he is in my prayers, as are Tanya, her baby, and the other girls. And I pray God will forgive me.

Though Momma and Daddy tell me I wasn't to blame for anything that happened, I feel in my heart that if I'd been stronger, and held Josh accountable when I first suspected something was wrong, the girls would have never been victimized by him.

Sometimes I dream that Josh and I are still married, that I'll wake up in his arms and everything will be the way it once was. Then I realize that it was only a dream all along. Our life together never was the fairytale I thought it to be.

THE END

STEPFATHER
How Can I Stop Him From Coming On To Me?

My mother and I both want the same man! I know that sounds kinky but it's true. Both of us were hung up on him, and I don't know what will become of our family once the truth is known!

I'm twenty years old and lived at home until my mother forced me to move out. My mother didn't know what was happening between my stepfather and me, and I damn sure wasn't going to tell her.

My real father deserted Mother and me when I was four. She worked as a nurse's aide while I was little, going to night classes to become a registered nurse. She worked hard and long, trying to make her life—and mine— much better.

"Someday you're going to live in a big house and have everything you want," she used to tell me as she bounced me on her knees.

"Will I have a new daddy?" I asked, innocently.

Mother would get a far away look and shake her head slowly. "Maybe sugar baby, but I can't promise you that."

I didn't understand what she meant but I smiled up at her, knowing my mother would take care of me, no matter what she had to do.

When I was seventeen my mother took a job at the local clinic. I'd just enrolled in nurse's aide classes at the local junior college, hoping to find a job nearby. One day, my mother came home bubbling over with excitement.

"Baby, guess what happened?" she asked.

She came up to me and held my hand.

"Dr. Spears at the clinic has asked me out. Can you believe that, child?"

Asked my mother out? I couldn't believe it. In all the years we'd been alone, she never once dated. It seemed she spent all her time either working or being with me.

"That's—uh—great," I replied. You know when I look back now I'm not really sure whether it was or not. I realized I was maturing into a woman but I still didn't want to let go of my mother.

"He's a wonderful man, sugar," she said, sitting down on the recliner and kicking off her shoes. "Just the kind of man I've always dreamed of."

I swallowed my pride and sat down next to her.

"Mom, I'm real happy for you. It's time you had a life of your own. Good luck!" I kissed her soft cheek.

She smiled and breathed a sigh of relief.

If she was happy then I was going to be happy. I owed that to my good mother.

Within a year, my mother and Dr. Spears were married. He was a wonderful man, sweet, kind and loving. I could tell by the way he always stared at her, he loved her very much.

By the time Warrington and she had been married almost a year, I graduated from school. I'd also found a young man who interested me and I thought my life was going along smoothly.

Charlie Wright was getting ready to transfer to a four-year college when we met. We spent the summer together hanging out at the beach and just plain goofing off.

"Where are you going to be working?" he asked one night as we sat on the beach watching the sunset.

"I've been offered a job at my stepfather's clinic. I start in September."

"Oh that's great," he complained with a sour expression on his face. "I was hoping you'd get a job closer to where I stay ... then I can see more of you."

I fixed my gaze at him while deep in thought. Charlie was a real cool guy and I hoped there was more to our relationship than just dating.

"Well, maybe after I get some experience I can move closer, but till then..." I let my voice trail off and stared straight in to his eyes.

He knew what I wanted.

"Honey, you like to tease me don't you?" he said, pushing me down onto the sand. It was a hot summer night and he was quick in snatching off the scanty bikini I wore.

He was an expert in untying the knots on it. He wriggled out of his swim shorts. I shuttered with pleasure when I felt the hot sand against my bottom.

"Oh, honey," I whispered, kissing him hard on the lips. I'd been wound up all night and was ready to go crazy with his carrying on!

"Don't talk, sugar," he said, exploring my body. Not an inch of it was left to suffer the feeling of being left out. His fingers were like a forest fire's roaring flames, consuming and driving into a throbbing, sexual frenzy. I wanted him to make wild passionate love to me.

It was dark, but the faint outline of a lighthouse provided enough light to watch the breakers. They'd lose their strength and become small waves and when they finally made their way to us, they tickled our toes.

He didn't let that stop his hungry hands. He let his lips burn into my soul and tenderly mouthed my erect peaks, my wriggling encouraging him more. I slid my hands up and down his back, feeling the tightness of the muscles he worked so hard to build. My fingers clutched his firm bottom and I squeezed gently. He was hard ... and he was ready.

"You're driving me crazy with your educated hands," he whispered in my ear. The darkness was like a cloak over us and we rolled back and forth enjoying our erotic areas and intimacy.

When his strong hands opened me to his desires, I held my breath. I hungered for him so desperately and relief was getting close! I positioned myself and felt him roll on top of me. I tensed, waiting for the stabbing pleasure and final release.

I felt his hardness against me and I was ready.

He moved with quickness, but not quick enough. A huge wave from the beach came crashing to shore and sent us floating up the beach.

"Oh!" he grumbled, snatching his swimsuit before the wave took it out to sea. "Perfect timing!"

I stared at us in the dim light from the lighthouse. We are dripping wet and I couldn't help feeling tickled.

This wasn't exactly the release I'd been waiting for!

Charlie helped me find my bikini. "That's okay sugar, there'll be other times."

I kissed him and nestled my face on his thick neck.

"I hope so darling ... but next time, let's stay a way from the beach!"

He swatted me playfully on the bottom and we splashed in the sand back to the car. I had enjoyed myself, despite the "watery" interruption.

Charlie went off to college and I went to work at the clinic. I didn't really warm up to my stepfather; I damn sure didn't want him to feel he owed me something special just because he married my mother. "Do you like it here, Desiree?" he asked one night as we were closing up the clinic. My mother had left earlier to go pick up drapes for our new house and we were the only ones left.

"Yes I do very much," I replied breathlessly, enjoying the mysterious, unexplored feelings between us. There was an alarm in the back of my mind that had made me keep my distance. I didn't want it to sound off, but I grew more and more curious as to what would make it go off. He was so very handsome in his white jacket. His gold-rim glasses were such a neat contrast to his dark skin. In this light tonight, he looked a bit like Billy Dee Williams, the movie star. He knew he was cool looking and he knew he didn't need to come on strong—he was utterly self-assured, and that's all that really mattered.

"Good," he said, moving closer, placing his had on mine. "I don't want you to ever leave the clinic. You're much too valuable."

His warm hand made my heart do flip-flops. My eyes traveled to his face and his intense gaze held me momentarily spellbound. The situation was making me feel very uncomfortable. He wasn't looking at me like a stepdaughter; he was looking at me like he wanted more than just small talk ... and I wasn't sure what to do.

"I've—uh er—gotta get going," I said, pushing past him. He reached out and grabbed my arm. I couldn't move . . . not because of the hold he had on me ... but because of the inner-power that was coming from him. It was like static electricity, crackling with sensuality.

He pulled me next to him and turned me around. His hand held my chin and I felt my heart beating like a pile driver in my chest. This was wrong! My mind was spinning and I couldn't resist him. I didn't want to!

Warrington was different than at home. He wasn't the medical professional who ran our household like he ran the clinic. This man was sexually starved, he was yearning for something I had to offer. But was I willing to give it to him?

I broke the spell.

"Stop it, you're acting crazy. What— er—what if Mom sees what is happening!" My voice didn't have the tone of sincerity but I knew that if he'd taken me into his arms right then, I'd have willingly surrendered to his touch.

"I'm only your stepfather," he said in a low, husky voice as smooth as silk. "I only want to get to—uh— know you better."

I stared into his eyes. Gone was the intense look of only a moment ago. In its place was the caring look of a man who was concerned about the feelings of his stepdaughter.

Had I read more into our meeting than was there? Did I feel the mysterious electricity that is only shared by lovers? Or, did I imagine what was happening, only to fulfill some fantasy really deep down in my heart?

I wasn't a psychology major but I did know when a man was coming on to me. And this was one of those times!

"I'll see you at home," I said sharply, reaching for my coat and leaving the office. "This won't ever happen again," I shot over my shoulder as I slammed the door.

Outside, I took a deep breath. I prayed my wishes were going to come true!

It seemed my mother was gone more than she was home. During the day she worked at the clinic but her nights were spent either shopping for her new house or going to the many clubs to which she suddenly belonged.

I didn't begrudge my mother her time alone. After all, she'd worked hard and for the first in a long time, was enjoying life. What bothered me was being alone with her husband.

"How are you feeling, honey?" he asked one night when my mother was at a women's club meeting.

I was in the kitchen, fixing a sandwich when he came up behind me and put his lips on my neck. His breath was hot against my skin and I felt myself yielding to his touch.

I realized what was happening and pulled away!

"I'm—uh—fine," I lied, moving across the kitchen. I knew I found myself attracted to him but never would I allow anything to happen between him and me. This was my stepfather for crying out loud!

He followed me to the table and sat down across from me. He cleared his throat and his dark eyes stared at me. I fingered my sandwich nervously not wanting to look at him.

"Desiree, you know what's happening don't you?"

I started to take a bite of the sandwich and started gagging on it. I sputtered and coughed and he was behind me ready to administer the Heimlich maneuver. I tried to push him away but his strong arms held me tight just below my heaving breasts.

I spit up the half-chewed bread before he was able to use the maneuver but he still held me tight. I was conscious of his strong arms around me. Where our bodies made contact I felt electricity run through my veins.

He was excited I could tell. His hardness was pressed against my bottom and I held my breath, afraid to make a move. What was going to happen? Was he going to let go of me? I knew better.

His lips scorched my neck and I found myself leaning against him enjoying his kisses. I realized I'd been slowly falling in love with him.

"You like this don't you, sugar?" he whispered, kissing my ear. What was happening? Did I want it to happen?

"Please don't." My words were useless. I was enjoying his touch and leading him on. I was acting like a shameless whore trying to make it with my mother's husband!

I savored his kisses and the intimacy of the moment. I leaned into his hard body and smelled his cologne. I closed my eyes and let his lips dance across my neck and face. He turned me slowly to face him and held my chin so he could look into my eyes.

"We both want this, don't we?" he growled in a deep, sexy voice dripping with passion

I wasn't sure! Was I that uncaring to think of my mother? I tried to look away but it was impossible. He put his hand on my shoulder and lowered his head.

I raised my lips only to come to my senses before we kissed!

"Don't!" I screamed, tearing myself from his hold. "This is wrong and you know it. Leave me alone or I'm telling my mother!"

His eyes grew wide and he laughed at me mockingly. "You cheap little bitch," he bellowed. "You want this as much as I do. So you wanna play games, huh?" He licked his lips slowly. "Well fine, because I'll be waiting for you to come crawling to me. You loved every minute of this and..." He reached down and stroked his manhood proudly, "you're gonna love this!"

His remark made me feel dirty and used; why was I still attracted? The last thing I wanted to do was betray my mother. She loved this man and didn't want my growing feelings of love mess up her life. I threw my sandwich in his face then started to march out of the kitchen.

"Wait a minute, girl," he ordered.

I turned and glared at him. "You filthy pig," I hissed, hating him for bringing out these feelings in me. "I—I meant what I said. Stay away from me!"

I ran out of the kitchen and up the stairs to my room.

Downstairs, he laughed at me like a crazy man.

I tried to stay away from my stepfather both at the clinic and at home. Every evening I tried to find something to do out of the house so I wouldn't be left alone with him. I bet I'm the only person who saw Robocop hundreds of times.

There were times while sitting in the movie theater when I thought about telling Charlie what was happening. What would I say—I found my stepfather sexually attractive? I decided not to say anything. This wasn't the kind of thing you discussed with your boyfriend!

"Warrington's going to a meeting tonight," my mother announced one evening after work. "I'm going over to the health club for a few hours. You won't mind being home alone, will you baby?"

"No," I answered simply. It was wonderful to be able to spend an evening at home without having to worry about my stepfather. "When will you be home?"

"Oh, before your stepfather gets home. You sure you don't mind?"

I took her hand and held it. I remembered the many nights she sat at home helping me with my homework, never dating just always being there for me. Now was her chance to enjoy life!

"You go on and have a good time. I'll be fine here, honestly!"

She smiled and kissed me on the cheek. I waved to her as she drove out of the driveway. Smiling to myself, I closed the door and locked it.

A whole evening to myself! I couldn't believe my luck! I wouldn't have to avoid contact with my stepfather I'd be able to take a hot bath and just goof off all evening.

I went into my bathroom and filled the tub with steamy, hot water and bubble bath. The bubbles filled the tub in no time. Taking off my clothes, I nestled down into the warm water and let all my tensions dissolve.

It was so comfortable being by myself. I closed my eyes and let my body relax. It was almost like being drugged and I didn't hear the bathroom door open.

"Taking a bath? You feeling dirty?"

I instantly recognized my stepfather's voice. My eyes flew open and I glared at him.

"Get outta here, right now!" I screamed, reaching for a towel. He got to it first and held it out.

"Come and get it, honey!"

"You filthy scum," I cried, stretching my hand out for the towel. I couldn't reach it. The only way was for me to get out of the tub.

Composing myself, I quickly stood up and stepped out of the tub and reached for the towel. I wasn't quick enough and found myself in his arms!

"What a nice surprise," he said, chuckling at my nakedness. "You're going to make this an enjoyable evening for me, aren't you sugar?"

"I told you to leave me alone," I protested, pushing him away. It didn't do any good. He scooped me into his arms and carried me to my bed. Unceremoniously, he dumped me on the spread.

"Play time!" was all he said as he stripped down to nothing. I looked at his muscular body and the hardness below. He wanted more than kisses. He lunged at me and pinned my arms above my head. "Don't fight me, sugar. We both want this."

His lips traveled across my cheeks, lingering on my mouth then moving down to my chest. He teased me with his kisses, sucking and claiming my body. I tried to fight him off but I couldn't. He was setting me on fire and I wanted him!

"Please..." I whispered not wanting to give into his touch. "What about Mom?" I felt a pang of guilt roll through me.

"Forget her, live for this!" His hands stroked the inside of my thighs and I found myself opening up to his hardness. He unpinned one of my arms and took my hand. "Feel me," he whispered as my fingers wrapped around his manhood. He was hard and hot ... and wanted me.

"Oh gawd," I cried, trying to fight back the urges building inside me. I didn't want him to stop. I knew I wasn't in love with him—it was only lust.

But I didn't have the strength to push him away!

I wanted what I held in my hand!

It became bare chest against bare chest as he joined me. I sucked in my breath, feeling his warm body above me. He was like an inferno, burning me with his every move.

I couldn't talk. All I felt was the urgency of his moves. Like a puppet I dangled from his string doing as he wished. I moved with him, letting my senses take control.

126

It didn't take long for the ultimate pleasure to come. I felt my body ripple slowly, then grow as a tidal wave of passion crashed on my beach.

I cried out from sheer ecstasy, and felt his body collapse on mine.

I couldn't move. I looked anxiously about the room and my eyes fell upon a picture of my mother. Suddenly, I felt sick and pushed hard on my stepfather.

"Get off me," I screamed, tearing his flesh with my nails. "You tricked me!"

"Ouch!" he yelled, rolling off me in one smooth movement. "You dirty bitch, look what you've done?" He ran his fingertips across the welts forming on his chest.

I rolled off the bed and put on my robe. I was trembling and my whole world seemed about to explode. I tried to control my nerves then spoke, my voice trembling.

"G-Get outta here, now! Wh-What we did—was—wrong!" Salty tears stung mat eyes and I watched him get dressed slowly. He took an extra long time zipping his pants and I looked away in shame. He was teasing me and I hated him for it!

"You liked it, sugar, and you know it!" He grinned at me then marched out of the room.

I couldn't stop shaking! He was right, I did enjoy it! But he'd taken advantage of me. He'd used his handsome natural charm to make me give in.

This was wrong and we both knew it. The only problem was that he wasn't going to let it go at this. He'd want more and I wasn't going to give him any more! He'd taken my body but not my mind! If he touched me again ... I swear I was going to kill him!

I keep my distance from my stepfather. It wasn't easy living in the same family and working with him, but I tried. I knew I had to find a place of my own and decided to move as soon as I'd saved enough money. Asking my mother for a loan was out of the question. She wanted me to stay at home and I couldn't tell her why I wanted to move!

Work was tough. Every time I was with my stepfather he'd make some remark. I was getting tired of listening to him but more than that, I was worried about the tone his voice was taking. He was threatening me without saying .a word. He'd make a remark then quickly mask it over with a clever word or two. He knew what he wanted all right—he wanted me!

The week before I was to go looking for an apartment, I found myself alone at home. I knew my mother was down at the corner Safeway doing her grocery shopping. I still hadn't told her about my wanting to move out. I'd saved almost enough and all I needed was one more paycheck.

My mother told me that Warrington was down at the gun club playing with his "toys." He collected guns like some boys collect baseball cards. I had the house all to myself.

I filled a bowl with chips and went into the den, which was sort of a family room. The TV was in there along with an assortment of guns Warrington collected. They were locked a wooden cabinet with a glass door.

I plopped down into the recliner and reached for the TV remote control. I was going to enjoy this evening alone.

"Whatcha lookin' at, honey?"

I cringed when I heard my stepfather's voice. Even from where I sat, I could smell the liquor on his breath. He'd been drinking and I knew I was in for trouble.

I jumped to my feet and cried, "You—you're supposed to be at the club."

He staggered toward me. He didn't look too steady on his feet and I anxiously waited for a chance to run past him.

"I—uh—wanted to see you, sugar," he said, his words slurred from the liquor he'd been drinking.

I held up my hands.

"Stay away from me," I cried, trying not to sound too hysterical. I was really afraid now and didn't know what to do.

He came towards me real quick and I jumped aside, knocking a small box to the floor. The top of the box opened and a small pistol fell onto the carpet.

I picked it up quickly and pointed at my stepfather.

"S-Stay away, or—I'll or I'll shoot," I warned just like in those silly late-night movies. Shit, I didn't even know if the gun was loaded; it felt heavy in my hands but I wasn't wise enough to see if it had bullets.

"Hey sugar," he said, sauntering up to me as steadily as his drunken legs would allow. "P-Put that gun down." He forced a stupid grin and I glared at him.

"I said stay away or I'll shoot!"

"You're full of shit, girl," he cried as he lunged for me. All I remember is the gun going off. The noise in the room was ear-splitting! I'd closed my eyes when I pulled the trigger, now I opened them quickly to see my stepfather lying on the floor, his pant soaked with blood.

"Oh no!" I cried, running to the phone and punching 9ll. I knew I hadn't killed him but his leg was bleeding pretty bad. And as much as I hated him, I couldn't let him bleed to death.

"You dirty slut!" he screamed, his eyes wide with pain. "You tried to kill me!"

"Shut up!" I screamed. I didn't want to hear his accusations. He forced me to shoot, just like he'd forced himself on me.

Within minutes the ambulance arrived. The paramedics put him on a stretcher and rolled him out of the house. A police officer was there and told me he was taking me down to the station.

"B-But it was an accident," I wailed, feeling my eyes floating in tears. "He came at me, officer. I—uh—wasn't going to kill him!"

The policeman tried to quiet me. "Calm down, this is only routine. All shootings must be investigated."

"That's great," I thought to myself. I didn't want my mother to know what was happening and now she'd find it all out. How was I going to face her when I told her I'd been attracted to her husband? Hadn't I fallen for his caresses? Wasn't my conscience the only thing keeping me from being in his bed again?

I felt dirty and cheap. I should've gone and talked to her but I didn't. Now, I had to face the consequences.

"What do you mean telling these lies, Desiree?" my mother scolded when I told her the truth. She didn't want to believe what I was telling her and she made it quite plain. "Men don't mess with women unless they lead them on, girl, and you know it!"

"But I didn't," I cried. "He made the first move. He wouldn't leave me alone. I found him attractive at first but when he wouldn't leave me alone I couldn't stand it any longer! I didn't want to hurt you! He was coming after me again and I shot him! I wasn't going to kill him, Mother!"

"Kill him Shit girl, my loving husband is lying in that hospital bed in shock Another inch and you'd have hit an artery. You've always hated him, haven't you'"

Hated him', I hadn't hated him. I thought kit:' I thought he was the best thing for my mother. Little good it did me. She was turning this around to like I was the guilty one.

"What does your husband say?" I asked, hoping to hear his side of the story.

My mother stiffened. "He says you've been after him for months and I don't mean in a lady-like way. You were flirting and carrying on. And poor 'Warrington ... having the urges like a natural man, couldn't push you away!" Her voice quivered with anger. "I-I'm ashamed to call you my daughter!"

I felt like she had slapped me. She believed his lies--all of them!

"Aw Mom," I cried, trying to reach out for her. She backed away like I was poison. "C'mon don't be like this. Believe me, I'm telling the truth. I love you and don't want to see you hurt."

She held me by my shoulders and looked me squarely in the eyes. "Girl, I've got to believe my husband. He says he's not pressing charges and told me to get you outta the house!" She handed me a check for a thousand dollars. "Get yourself your own place and don't come by making any more trouble."

I took the check and stared at it. So this was it! I thought my mother and I had a good understanding of each other. Apparently, I was wrong. She was willing to pay to get rid of me!

"I'll have my clothes out tonight," I said, my voice dropping to a whisper.

She squared her shoulders and looked at me. "Good, now I'm going back to my husband."

She stood and marched down the hall to his room.

I walked out of her life.

A year has gone by and I'm doing real well. I stayed on at the clinic for a few weeks until I was offered a job at the hospital. I work with children now so I hardly see Warrington when he's on his rounds.

Charlie, my old boyfriend is coming to spend a long weekend with me in my new apartment. We've been writing and he's called several times to check on me. I told him what happened, and he's been really understanding!

As for my mother, well, I'd like to say we're friends again, but that hasn't happened. We talk about once a week but. She has her life and I have mine. I think we'll be close again some day, but I don't know when.

Maybe my mother and I will be friends again when Warrington moves onto his next conquest.

I sure hope so! My future looks good and I want my mother's to be the same!

THE END